Twe...
Twelve ...
One UNIFO... ...series.

Don't miss a story in Harlequin Blaze's
12-book continuity series featuring irresistible
soldiers from all branches of the armed forces.

Now serving—
those ready and able heroes in the U.S. Navy...

HIGHLY CHARGED!
by Joanne Rock
April 2011

HIGH STAKES SEDUCTION
by Lori Wilde
May 2011

TERMS OF SURRENDER
by Leslie Kelly
June 2011

Uniformly Hot!—
The Few. The Proud. The Sexy as Hell!

Blaze

Dear Reader,

Don't you just love a man in uniform?

There's something so sexy about a strong, powerful guy whose clothes proclaim him to be a hero. Especially if his words and actions back it up.

I live in Maryland, not far from Annapolis, and there have been many spring days when I've seen that town filled to the brim with handsome young students from the Naval Academy, clad in their dress whites. Believe me, these "Middies" are a featured attraction.

I hope you enjoy Danny and Marissa's story. Danny is my kind of hero—smart, sexy, charming, loyal. In this story, it was the heroine who had to prove to me that she was worthy of the hero, and I think she did.

While you're reading, please be on the lookout for one of my favorite characters: Brionne, the heroine's adorable cat. Brionne is actually based on a real-life furry friend who's looking for a forever home (she really does play fetch!). If you're an animal lover—like so many of the Blaze authors are—please check out blazeauthors.com to find out about our new Pet Project!

Best wishes and happy reading!

Leslie Kelly

Leslie Kelly

TERMS OF SURRENDER

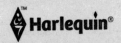
Harlequin®

TORONTO NEW YORK LONDON
AMSTERDAM PARIS SYDNEY HAMBURG
STOCKHOLM ATHENS TOKYO MILAN MADRID
PRAGUE WARSAW BUDAPEST AUCKLAND

If you purchased this book without a cover you should be aware that this book is stolen property. It was reported as "unsold and destroyed" to the publisher, and neither the author nor the publisher has received any payment for this "stripped book."

Recycling programs
for this product may
not exist in your area.

ISBN-13: 978-0-373-79620-5

TERMS OF SURRENDER

Copyright © 2011 by Leslie A. Kelly

All rights reserved. Except for use in any review, the reproduction or utilization of this work in whole or in part in any form by any electronic, mechanical or other means, now known or hereafter invented, including xerography, photocopying and recording, or in any information storage or retrieval system, is forbidden without the written permission of the publisher, Harlequin Enterprises Limited, 225 Duncan Mill Road, Don Mills, Ontario, Canada M3B 3K9.

This is a work of fiction. Names, characters, places and incidents are either the product of the author's imagination or are used fictitiously, and any resemblance to actual persons, living or dead, business establishments, events or locales is entirely coincidental.

This edition published by arrangement with Harlequin Books S.A.

For questions and comments about the quality of this book please contact us at Customer_eCare@Harlequin.ca.

® and TM are trademarks of the publisher. Trademarks indicated with ® are registered in the United States Patent and Trademark Office, the Canadian Trade Marks Office and in other countries.

www.Harlequin.com

Printed in U.S.A.

ABOUT THE AUTHOR

Leslie Kelly has written dozens of books and novellas for Harlequin Blaze, Temptation and HQN. Known for her sparkling dialogue, fun characters and depth of emotion, her books have been honored with numerous awards, including the National Readers' Choice Award, the *RT Book Reviews* Award, and three nominations for the highest award in romance, the RWA RITA®. Leslie resides in Maryland with her own romantic hero, Bruce, and their three daughters. Visit her online at www.lesliekelly.com.

Books by Leslie Kelly

HARLEQUIN BLAZE

347—OVEREXPOSED
369—ONE WILD WEDDING NIGHT
402—SLOW HANDS
408—HEATED RUSH
447—BLAZING BEDTIME STORIES
     "My, What a Big...You Have!"
501—MORE BLAZING BEDTIME STORIES
     "Once Upon a Mattress"
521—PLAY WITH ME
537—BLAZING BEDTIME STORIES, VOLUME V
     "A Prince of a Guy"
567—ANOTHER WILD WEDDING NIGHT

To get the inside scoop on Harlequin Blaze and its talented writers, be sure to check out blazeauthors.com.

Don't miss any of our special offers. Write to us at the following address for information on our newest releases.

Harlequin Reader Service
U.S.: 3010 Walden Ave., P.O. Box 1325, Buffalo, NY 14269
Canadian: P.O. Box 609, Fort Erie, Ont. L2A 5X3

To Brenda.
I can't say it enough but I'll just keep trying.
Thank you.

Prologue

Friday 5/6/11, 07:00 a.m.
www.mad-mari.com/2011/05/06/friday-contest
Happy Friday!

Those of you who are regulars here at Mad-Mari.com know I belong to the I-love-Fridays cult. Not just because it's the end of the work week (except for me, the unemployed, but more on that later) but because it's my favorite day here on the blog. Every Friday, I invite you to share tales of your bad dates from last weekend, and we all get to spend the day thinking how great it is that ours aren't the only love lives that suck. Wahoo!

You know the drill, just leave a comment, describing how bad things were on your last date. Most entertaining story—decided solely by me, 'cause, I am master of this here e-universe—gets an autographed copy of my new book.

Now, a bit of good news for me, which might be bad news for you, depending on how much you like to hang out here on my blog. Tomorrow, I actually have a job interview. For a real job. In the real world. AK!

Okay, it's not permanent—just a summer gig. But I can't tell you how much I need it. To answer the question before you ask—no, my two books have not made me rich. Some men just don't seem to get my humor, plus I have a lot of student loans to pay off. (And no, for the last time, I'm not telling you where I went to school, or what I studied. Trust me. It's boring.)

I plan to spend the day getting prepped—touching up the résumé, brushing up on interview etiquette, plucking my eyebrows. (Ow!) So you all feel free to talk about those bad dates and I'll check in later tonight, okay?

P.S. Thought for the day: Is it better to be unemployed and happy, or have a good-paying job you hate? Discuss!

Friday 5/6/11, 11:15 p.m.
www.mad-mari.com/2011/05/06/friday-contest
Comment #114
Promised I'd check in! I'm about to hit the hay but wanted to choose a winner from today's sucky-date contest.

Rachel from Boston wins an autographed copy of one of my books. Sorry to everyone else who entered, but I can't even imagine what it was like to go on a date with a crazy dude whose opening line was, "I like to sneak into my mother's room, steal her panties and dance around in them, like I'm Britney Spears."

Uhh...eww.

Rachel, honey? Please tell me you didn't let this

guy know where you live. If you did, I hope you have a fresh supply of mace. And antibacterial soap. And a lock on your underwear drawer.

Hmm. What's more disturbing about this story? A grown man's mother having Britney Spears-ish panties, or her son wearing them?

Okay, gotta run. Please wish me luck on the job interview tomorrow. Can't tell you more about it—as you know, I like to keep my Mad-Mari stuff on the down low, separate from my real world junk.

But trust me, this job? Well, let's just say it involves me swimming in a huge sea of testosterone.

Here I go…diving in!

Mari

1

MARISSA MARSHALL LOVED clear, sunny spring days, and, so far, this early May one was reminding her why.

Having lived in Baltimore for five years, she was used to gray, smoggy skies during the cold, bleak winter, and hazy ones in the summer. Fall was nice, with changing leaves ranging from pale yellow to deep rust. But in spring, Maryland came alive.

There was so much color. Cherry blossoms and azaleas dotted the landscape with pink and red. Lush farmlands erupted in mixed tones of new, freshly turned earth. With the soft green waters of the Atlantic, and the warm yellow sun drenching the robin's-egg-blue sky with life, the state was an artist's palette.

Funny, though. Her favorite part of spring—the color she most enjoyed on a beautiful day like this—was no color at all.

It was white. Just white. A sea of it.

"Dazzling," Marissa said. Though she'd been speaking to a woman behind the counter of the coffee shop where she'd stopped for a caffeine injection, she was looking out the window.

Students from the U.S. Naval Academy, wearing their immaculate uniforms, filled the streets of Annapolis. Though now coed, the USNA's student body was primarily male. So on this lovely Saturday afternoon, the town appeared full to the brim of handsome young midshipmen—aka middies—in their dress whites, all celebrating making it through another tough year at the academy.

Women from all over the state flocked here on sunny spring days, just to have a good drool. Marissa among them.

"God, how can you survive this much hotness 24/7?"

The woman grunted. "They're always broke. I don't care how hot they are, I just wonder if they have cash in their pockets."

Marissa would probably wonder less about the contents of their pockets and more about what was in the *rest* of their pants. Anyone who didn't have something dangling in their own pants would. As would danglers with same-sex preferences.

The USNA might be renowned for its educational excellence, but a close second would have to be its military beefcake. Even Marissa, who had been single for so long she could call herself a sexual vegetarian, suddenly found herself craving a Manwich.

She knew better than to ever take a bite, though. Uniformed beefcake might taste good, but the thought of that uniform got stuck in her craw, choking her. She might like looking at them, but she had no use for military men. Not after having been sired by one. Her father was about as affectionate as a jellyfish.

Besides, lately, even men without uniforms had been few and far between. That, however, was her own fault.

In her real life, she was an overeducated nerd who'd just completed a doctoral program from one of the most prestigious universities in the country—Johns Hopkins. So she intimidated most men.

In her secret life, she was persona non grata with the male half of civilization due to her snarky books: *Why Do Men Suck?* and *Thanks, But I'll Just Keep My Vibrator.*

How strange that her blog, Mad-Mari.com, which she'd launched six years ago after a really bad date, had landed her here. What had started as an internet rant had grown into a website with tons of followers. Then came a book deal.

As Mad-Mari, she was sassy and irreverent while venting about the hell called dating and relationships. She'd railed against cheaters, chauvinists and misogynistic assholes. She'd met lots of those in academia, not to mention in the military world in which she'd been raised. Meanwhile, she'd also been writing her much more proper, respectable dissertation which touched on similar topics, just in a scholarly, scientific way.

In other words, no snark.

Thankfully, she'd published the books under a pseudonym. Very few people realized that the infamous man-bashing internet star, Mad-Mari, was really Marissa Marshall, PhD, whose dissertation had been excerpted in a highly respected psychology journal and in a military magazine. And she intended to keep it that way.

The barista set a cup on the counter. "Honestly, I've never been tempted to trade in my granny panties for something with cougar stripes—they're practically babies."

They might be babies next to the fiftyish server, but not to Marissa. The oldest cadets were twenty-three or so, not that far from her twenty-nine. But in terms of life experience, they were a different generation. From age fourteen, Marissa had been thrust into adulthood, nearly raising her own younger siblings.

There hadn't been much choice after their mother left.

While studying to earn her doctorate in psychology, she'd spent a lot of time trying to understand that. If pressed, she'd probably have to admit that trying to understand what drove people like her parents to do the things they did was one reason she'd settled on psychology from the day she'd started college.

Oh, she got why the marriage had failed—her father was one of those chauvinistic misogynists she wrote about, cold and aloof. Not to mention a cheat, seeming to have a new affair on every base. But she couldn't grasp how a mother could decide to pay him back by having an affair of her own, then leave her kids, keeping in touch only with an occasional call or card. Some things, she suspected, she would never understand, no matter how many degrees she earned or how many letters came after her name.

"You have a good day. Try not to trip and fall into a pile of hot boys now, ya hear?" said the woman behind the counter.

Not impossible, given her three-inch heels. "Thanks."

Stepping outside, she instinctively closed her eyes and sucked in a deep breath. She lived near the Inner Harbor, but the air didn't smell nearly as potent. Downtown Baltimore lacked this fragrant mixture of saltwater, sweat and *male*.

"Excuse me, ma'am," a deep voice said.

Her eyes flying open, she saw a twentyish guy, dressed

all in white. Marissa had stepped right into his path. "My fault."

Then something sunk in. He'd called her *ma'am*.

"Ma'am?" she mumbled. The professor under whom Marissa had interned was a ma'am. Her elderly neighbor, whose apartment always smelled like pickled beets, *she* was a ma'am. But Marissa?

When, by God, did I become a ma'am?

"Today, that's a good thing," she told herself. Today, she wanted to convey seriousness, maturity. Ma'am-ness. Today she was not Mad-Mari, she was Dr. Marissa Marshall. Even if she didn't yet know who that was, other than a name on a résumé.

It was time to find out. Some people said going to school for so long and making a living by writing sassy words in the comfort of her own living room had been her means of escaping the reality of adulthood. Well, her best friend said it. And maybe her favorite college professor had, too.

Maybe she *had* been putting off the inevitable. Maybe the newly degreed shrink in her head was right in suspecting she'd been so sick of being forced to be an adult when she was a teenager that she'd needed to drop all responsibilities and focus only on herself during her twenties.

But that was over. She was ready for whatever came next, ready for part two of her life. Her blog and her books had been fun. They'd been stress relievers during her all-men-suck period (hence the title of her book). But she was a professional now. Time to put away the snark and move forward.

That's why her hair was pulled back in a severe bun. That's why she'd dressed in a simple blouse and a borrowed skirt—her own clothes being far too Mad-Mari-ish for Marissa Marshall. That's why she wore painful black pumps, more appropriate for a funeral in January than an appointment at the USNA in May. That's why she had actually contorted herself into a pair of pantyhose for the first time in several years.

Because today, she would be meeting with a Deputy to the Commandant of the Midshipmen, to convince him to hire her to give some guest lectures on campus. She needed the work. She needed the professional credit. And frankly, she needed the money.

Her royalties on her first book had been eaten up by tuition—Johns Hopkins was in no way cheap. The advance on her second book had been keeping her fed, but it was almost gone. There should be more coming in, but, in publishing, money flowed with the speed of sap off an elm. Whatever else she earned she would use to hang out her counseling shingle. For now, though, she couldn't afford insurance, much less office space.

So hearing from her former professor that the USNA was interested in talking to her about doing a few guest lectures for summer students had been a lifeline tossed when she'd been trying to decide between her cell phone and her cable-TV bills. The phone was important. But she wasn't sure she could give up her Starz Channel dates with the hot gladiators on *Spartacus*.

"Okay, gotta nail this," she said as she got into her car.

Reaching for her notebook, she read over the details for the interview. "King George Street to Gate 1," she mumbled. "First meeting at two, check in with security an hour before."

Oh, God. How had she forgotten that? She'd been so focused on preparing for the interview, she'd neglected the details!

"You idiot," she howled, eyeing the clock. Five 'til one.

Thrusting the key in the ignition, she prayed the car—which had been giving her trouble—would start easily. Fortunately, it groaned only once, then fired up.

Using a lead foot on the gas pedal, she got to the academy in a few minutes. Spying the correct building and the Employees Only lot in front, she weighed her options. The lot was almost empty, so she wouldn't be taking anybody's spot. Plus, if she had her way, she would be an employee this summer.

Decision made. Parking quickly, she exited the car, pausing to retuck her blouse and smooth her skirt. The pantyhose were beyond annoying, and she took a second to try to twist them into position. Which just tugged her panties into the *wrong* position.

"Oh, for God's sake," she whispered, feeling the elastic panty line riding *way* too high on one cheek. Her too-tight skirt probably magnified the thing like a microscope did an amoeba.

Marissa did the wedgie-dance, wishing she wore thongs—it felt like she was wearing one, anyway. Better yet, she should have scraped up the money for new clothes that fit better. But the interview had come up suddenly and a borrowed skirt in her size had sounded fine, until she'd put it on this morning. It seemed the months of writing at home had added to her waistline, not to mention her hips and butt. The long pencil skirt fit like a casing on a sausage. And the sausage was trying to escape.

She tried tugging, keeping her backside toward the interior of the car so nobody would be able to see from the windows fronting the lot. But it didn't help much. Her inner Dr. Marshall told her to just forget it and hope nobody noticed the obnoxious panty lines. But, damn, she did not want some military man eyeing her tush any more than necessary in the tight skirt.

Then…disaster. She tugged too hard, and felt the whispery sensation of a run sliding down the length of one leg. She looked down to see a thick, ugly line appear at her knee and keep right on going until it disappeared into her shoe. "Shit!"

Panty lines were one thing. A huge freaking run down her shin? Was she just destined to not get this job?

Do something!

There was only one choice. Knowing she might not have a chance to hit a ladies' room inside, she bent back into the car, perching on the edge of the driver's seat, her feet out on the blacktop. She cast one more look around, still seeing nobody.

Pulling the door close to her legs, she wriggled the hose off, contorting herself into a ladle shape to tug them out from under the long, slim skirt.

She took the panties, too.

Commando might be more of a Mad-Mari thing, but panty lines would be even more obnoxious without the hose to smooth things out. The skirt was long; she didn't worry about flashing anyone.

She wadded up the ball of satin and nylon, stuffed it into the glove box, and stepped back out onto the blacktop seconds later. Runless. Wedgieless. Not to mention pantyless.

"That's probably not a good idea."

She yelped. Shocked by the intrusion of a deep voice, Marissa swung around, her heart thudding in her chest and her face going up in flames.

Outside the nearest building—a huge one with roll-up doors—stood a man. He watched her, a slight smile on his face. He hadn't been there a few minutes ago when she'd pulled up, and she had to wonder when he'd appeared, and how much he'd seen.

You were hidden by the door, dummy. No way could he see you, especially below the waist.

Except, of course, her feet had been sticking out. And they'd been encircled by nylon and black satin for a couple of seconds. Oh, and there was the fact that she'd been fiddling with her underwear before clambering back into the car.

He knew. He had to know. She'd been busted like a kindergartener raiding the candy jar. Worse—picking her...seat.

Brazen it out.

Her chin went up and she pretended not to hear him. When she took a step away from the vehicle, he called out, "Uh, miss, seriously, you might want to rethink that."

Grr. She'd already rethought it, especially with the hint of coolness in the spring air creeping up her thighs. And higher.

"That could get you into some trouble," the man added.

Gritting her teeth, she said, "Oh, were you talking to me?"

The man, who wore faded mechanic's coveralls, approached her, wiping his greasy hands on a towel. His expression was impassive, a friendly smile not indicating what he was thinking.

That was okay, Mari had enough thoughts for both of them.

She gawked, making a mental note with every step he took.

Step: *Tall.*

Step: *Strong, with broad shoulders and thick arms straining against the faded fabric of his clothes.*

Step: *Lean-hipped and slim-waisted.*

Step: *Long, powerful legs that ate up the pavement.*

Step: *Great smile, broadening as he drew closer… and oh, a dimple in one cheek!*

Step, step, step: *Sexy, confident, gorgeous.*

How incredibly embarrassing that he could be coming over to tell her he'd seen London and France when she'd done her front-seat striptease. Though, not as bad as it would be if he told her he'd seen the Netherlands.

She told herself to cool it. Maybe he just wanted to say hi. Or he could be coming over to tell her he'd heard the roughness of her car's engine. Given the way he was dressed, and that he'd come out of a building that was obviously some kind of repair shop, she'd pegged him for a mechanic.

Maybe he needed to know the time. Or to tell her the whole place had been evacuated for a fire drill.

Say anything except I know you're not wearing any panties.

Not only because it would be embarrassing if he confirmed he'd seen her, but because it was such a sleazy, slimy come-on. And she didn't want to think this stranger—this very sexy man—had a sleazy bone in his body. That would probably break her long-single, brittle heart completely. Guys this handsome simply shouldn't be allowed to be scumbags.

Reaching her, the man studied her from behind his sunglasses, which were necessitated by the bright sunshine that painted the tips of his light brown hair gold. She couldn't help wondering what color his eyes were. Warm chocolate? Jade green? Something dazzling, she imagined. Because only a perfect set of eyes belonged in that face, with its high cheekbones, strong jutting jaw and broad, sensual mouth.

Masculine. That was the only word to describe him.

"Afternoon," he said pleasantly, as if they'd just been introduced at a social event, as if he wasn't standing there, thinking about her being pantyless.

Maybe he's not.

Yeah. Right.

"Hello," she mumbled.

He pushed the sunglasses up onto the top of his head with the tip of his finger. *Oh, my.* Not brown, not gold… something in-between. Like fine, clear amber. Absolutely beautiful.

"Wow," she whispered.

He heard. Because now those eyes were twinkling. Definitely twinkling. She'd heard the expression, but always figured it for an exaggeration. It wasn't. This guy had *you-can-trust-me-I'm-adorable* written on his very eyeballs.

"You look a little lost," he said, that deep voice friendly, matching the twinkle and his small smile.

"I'm fine, thank you."

"Are you sure? Maybe I can help. I know my way around."

A quick glance at the stitching on his chest revealed the name of a popular auto-repair chain: Midas. They must make a lot of house calls to the academy if he was so familiar with it.

Funny that he worked for a company with a name that suited him so well, given those gold highlights in his hair. She only wondered if his big, powerful hands had the golden touch. And what lucky woman was on the receiving end of it.

One thing was sure, he was nothing like the men she

usually associated with. There wasn't a professor-ish feature on him. Probably in his early- to-mid-thirties, he was all man, not boyish, despite the twinkle and the dimples. He was rugged, not a smoothly put-together package like a slick high-rise, but a naturally spectacular formation like…the Grand Canyon.

Okay, that was a little overdone, but still, the guy was robbing her of coherent thought. She could only look at him for another long moment, pretending to consider his offer.

His cheeks were slightly stubbled, a faint smear of grease visible beside his strong nose. His skin was bronzed, his hands calloused, his muscles, she would bet, coming from hard work, not from a fitness club. And the mouth. Oh, did the man have a mouth—all soft, sensuous, smiling lips.

A shiver moved throughout her entire body, so delicate she almost didn't notice. It took her a second to realize that shiver had been a pure, feminine response to him: attraction. Major attraction. She was no longer calculating how good-looking he was, her gears had shifted smoothly from *assess* to *covet*.

Stop it. It had been far too long since she'd been in a relationship if a guy who'd peeping-Tom'd her when she'd pulled off her underwear was giving her the shivers.

He didn't peeping-Tom you…you Sharon Stone'd him!

She tried to pull her thoughts together, determined not to give him an opening to make a sleazy remark. "I'm okay, thanks."

"Well, you might not need any help, but I gotta say, you're really tempting fate."

Curious about why, but afraid of how he'd answer,

she instead replied, "Thanks for your concern, but I'm not worried."

"Rule-breaker, huh?"

"No."

"Just like to live dangerously?"

Oh, hell. That cemented it, reminding her of why he'd come over here. He'd definitely seen her strip. "Not in the least."

"Well, I'll admit you don't look the type."

Her spine stiffened. "What's that supposed to mean?"

Gesturing toward her hair, then her clothes, he said, "I mean, you look more like a schoolteacher than a rebel."

That was a good thing. "That's the plan," she mumbled.

"You're not really a teacher, are you?" he asked.

"Not yet." She glanced at her watch. "Oh, damn it."

"You're late."

"How did you ever guess?" she asked, her tone dry.

There went the twinkle. And the dimple. And a broad, white grin. "'Cause you sped in here like demons were on your tail."

At least he hadn't said, *Demons were on your* naked *tail*.

"Yes," she admitted. "I have an interview. It's fifty minutes from now and they said to check in an hour early."

He waved a hand, unconcerned. "They tell everyone that. But the place is nearly deserted. It won't take you ten minutes to get the visitor's pass, I promise. Don't worry about it."

"Still, I don't want to risk it, so if you'll excuse me…"

"So you're worried about making a bad impression?"

Blowing out an impatient breath as he stopped her from turning away with just that amused tone in his voice, she admitted, "Yes, okay? Yes, I am."

"Well, I hate to break it to you, but you're not doing very well so far." He pointed to a nearby building. "Personnel offices have a bird's-eye view of this parking lot."

Oh, great. Was he saying that he wasn't the only one who had seen her doing her impromptu striptease? Catching her bottom lip between her teeth, she looked up at the windows, then down at her car, trying to judge the angle. Geometry wasn't her strongest suit, but it didn't seem utterly impossible that somebody looking down might have seen as much as this guy had. Plus, she had a sunroof.

"This is bad," she whispered.

"It's okay, you can handle it. If anybody says anything, just tell them you were worried about making it on time."

Gawking, she snapped, "Most people would be too polite to *say* anything."

"What does politeness have to do with it?"

"A gentleman wouldn't put me on the spot about this."

He crossed his arms over his chest. "You mean I wasn't being a gentleman? My mom'll be crushed."

If there had been any snarkiness in his voice, she might have been annoyed, but something about his charm was getting around her defenses. So far, he *had* been gentlemanly in trying to let her know he'd seen her stripping off her underclothes in broad daylight in a public parking lot.

"Look, I had a run," she explained, her tone grudging.

He glanced down. "In those heels?"

"Down one whole leg."

"I thought both legs were usually required for running."

She managed not to groan, realizing he thought she'd gone *for* a run. "I had a run in my pantyhose, okay?"

His gaze remained downward, and his voice was the tiniest bit husky when he said, "No big loss. You definitely don't need 'em. You have great legs."

Her cheeks warmed. The way he said that indicated he was a leg man. That in itself was refreshing, as most men she knew professionally were interested only in her academic credentials. And the few she met when at a bar or a party were all focused on the two appendages sticking out the front of her body, not the two at the bottom. *Hmm. Are breasts appendages?*

"Thanks. But the point is, I'm late, I want to make a good impression and I didn't have time to stop and buy hose."

He finally got it. "Ahh. That's why you did it?"

Wondering how pink her cheeks were, she mumbled, "Yes."

Smiling, he replied, "Well, luckily, I was here to see."

She gasped. Had he really just said that? Seriously, had he just admitted he'd been *lucky* enough to catch a crotch-shot from a complete stranger?

"Because, like I said, you really don't have to sweat the time. So you can go ahead and take care of this."

"Take care of it?" she asked. What? Did he think she was going to run back and magically produce new pantyhose from her purse, like a rabbit out of a hat, and put them on?

"Sure. Just get back in your car. I'll help you out."

Her jaw dropped open. "Uh…"

"I mean, if you need some directions, I can hop in the passenger seat and show you."

Directions? She'd bet he knew a lot about women's underwear and could give directions on how to get in—or *out*—of them.

The very thought of that reminded her again that she wasn't wearing anything under her skirt; that cool spring breeze flitting up her legs now felt a bit warmer.

The man did put off some serious heat.

She suddenly acknowledged the second big danger of going commando—aside from possibly getting caught. Getting aroused.

No, not aroused. But aware. Very, *very* aware.

He gestured down at his clothes. "That is, if you don't mind getting in close quarters with somebody so dirty."

She gulped, more confused than ever. Was this guy intentionally playing word games? Was he propositioning her…or teasing her? Being flirtatious, or serious? Was she just being dirty-minded when thinking about how he'd said the word *dirty?*

"I'm not following," she said.

Appearing sympathetic, he explained, "You look stressed and nervous. Let's just get in the car and eliminate some of that tension before you go inside."

Relieve her stress. Her tension.

There was one surefire way to do that. Hmm. Maybe that explained why she'd been stressed for thirteen months, two weeks and four days. Oh, and seven hours. But who was counting how long it had been since she'd been laid? Though, she supposed writing a dissertation had been pretty stressful, too. At least, that's what the last guy she'd been involved with had thought. He'd stopped calling around the time she hit page one-twenty and officially lost her mind. Well, unofficially lost it—diagnosing yourself was a no-no in her line of work.

"Come on, let's just do it. You're running out of time, and you know you'll feel better afterward."

There. He'd stopped beating around the bush and suggested they do it. *It,* it. There had been no suggestive wag of the eyebrows, but what else could he mean? They'd moved beyond flirting and pantyhose. This complete stranger *was* proposing he help her relieve her tension by having sex in her car.

"It'll just take a couple of minutes."

If he did mean *it* it, she couldn't help wondering why he'd brag about *it* being over so fast. But she didn't wonder long; mainly she just felt disappointed. Yeah, she'd been distracted by his sexy wickedness for a moment or two. But now she could only feel punched in the gut by disappointment. He hadn't gone for the cheap line right away, but he'd still managed to come up with a sleazy suggestion eventually.

He might look like a blue-collar Prince Charming, but he was just another guy playing a game of follow-the-leader with his own dick.

"I don't think so. Heaven forbid *it* take longer than you think," she said, keeping her chin up and her eyes narrowed.

Marissa turned to walk away, already wondering how long she'd be thinking about those twinkling amber eyes and that incredibly sexy smile. Would she stop wondering what it might be like to kiss those perfect lips with the words that had emerged from them ringing in her ear?

"Okay, it's your wallet."

She paused midstep, glancing back at him. "My wallet?"

"Sure. The towing charge is $250.00."

Utterly confused, she turned around completely. "What on earth are you talking about?"

He pointed to a nearby sign. The one that said, "Employee Parking Only." In the small print beneath were a few more words: "Violaters Will Be Towed At Owner's Expense."

"They're real Nazis about it, even when the lot's practically empty."

Oh. My. God.

"Like I said, getting your car towed out of here during your interview wouldn't make the best first impression. And I promise, you do have time to move it. This place is pretty dead. I really don't mind escorting you to the closest public lot."

"You've got to be kidding me," she whispered. "You were talking about my car? About where I was parked?"

"Of course." Then, suddenly realizing the same thing she had—that they'd been having two different conversations—the sexy guy quirked a brow and tilted his head.

"What, exactly, were *you* talking about?"

THE BLONDE WITH THE scraped-back hair, the uplifted chin and the irritated expression was looking at him like he'd sprouted a set of wings out of his back. And while Lieutenant Commander Danny Wilkes did love to fly, he really couldn't manage it without the aid of an F/A-18 Hornet. Even the most experienced Naval Aviators couldn't, as far as he knew.

She didn't answer, merely staring at him with those

huge blue eyes, framed with the thickest lashes he'd ever seen. They fluttered as she blinked rapidly, like she was confused, trying to think of what to say. Considering he suspected the two of them had been engaging in totally different conversations, he figured he'd give her a little time to get herself together.

Not physically, of course. Oh, she was already together in that regard.

Funny, ever since he'd caught sight of her a few minutes ago, he'd had the refrain from Van Halen's *Hot For Teacher* going through his head. Even before she'd confirmed she was here to interview for a teaching position, she'd just come across as that cross of übersmart and supersexy. Like the fantasy ninth grade science teacher he'd never had.

He didn't know about the übersmart yet—so far their brief interaction had been a little odd, and she hadn't been at her conversational best.

But supersexy? *Hell, yeah.*

Her hair was pulled back into a severe bun, but that didn't mean he couldn't imagine what the thick, ash-blond strands would look like falling in a curtain over her shoulders. He'd already noticed the deep blue eyes, but had put away any blue-eyed-blonde-bimbo associations the minute she'd lifted her chin and frowned at him.

There was something sharp about her—a little edgy. He hadn't seen a single pouty look on her pretty face, nor one heavy-lidded, come-hither stare. And she hadn't walked or stood in a way that emphasized her curves, sending silent signals every guy learned to recognize by the age of fourteen.

Those curves. Oh, he'd definitely noticed those. He couldn't help but notice. He'd been openly admiring her slim calves while wondering about the long length of thigh he couldn't see beneath her skirt.

The clothes might be perfectly respectable—demure, in fact, at least if you looked up the definition of *skirt* and *blouse* in the dictionary. But not the way she wore them. The way the skirt hugged every inch of curvy hip and perfect backside, and the afternoon breeze molded her silky blouse against her slim shoulders and full, pert-tipped breasts, made her outfit rank right up there with anything out of Frederick's of Hollywood.

Sexy and prim, forward and flustered, unsure and determined. All in all, she was a contradictory puzzle—the most interesting one to cross his path in a very long time.

Right now, the only word to describe her was *confused*. The woman was staring at him, her eyes only slightly rounder than her mouth. It was as if he'd said something incomprehensible.

"Towed?"

He nodded, wondering if he should rethink that smart idea. She seemed to have trouble following a simple conversation. "Yeah. Towed. And then they ransom your car back to you for a ridiculous amount of money. They do it all the time. I think that's how they're going to fund the next generation of battleships."

Her mouth snapped shut, her bottom lip disappearing between her teeth for a second. She raised her hand to her face, covering her mouth. Then a sound emerged. A chuckle. Followed by another one. Her eyes sparkled with amusement and she slowly shook her head back and forth.

Danny's own smile widened. They'd apparently been crossing signals and he trusted she'd soon let him in on the joke. He felt even more sure of that when she dropped her hand and her chuckles turned into snorts of laughter.

"I'm such an idiot."

"You gonna tell me what we were really talking about?"

"Not on your life."

Ooh. Interesting. Very interesting. He quickly ran over their conversation in his mind, trying to find anything outrageous, but for the life of him, he just couldn't do it. He'd asked if she wanted to make a good impression and pointed out the window, she'd admitted she was in a hurry, he'd suggested she take a minute to move her car. What could be more innocent?

Except, the dirty part. But, she couldn't have thought he meant…no. This teacher-type wouldn't mentally go there.

Her eyes were now damp with what looked like tears of laughter. Her expression had gone from amused to embarrassed.

Okay. Maybe she *had* gone there.

"Did you think I was propositioning you? That I wanted to get you in your car to…"

Looking almost sheepish, she slowly nodded.

"Wow," he said, running a hand through his hair. "I've been told I sometimes move a little fast. But believe me, I do not usually meet a woman, and, five minutes later, tell her she oughta do me in the backseat of her car."

Another grin. "Your mom definitely wouldn't think you were gentlemanly if you did that."

"My dad would be the one who'd whack me one if I ever did such a thing. And my baby sister would kick my ass."

Her chuckles finally died, though her smile remained. That smile made her look younger, softer. Made her blue eyes gleam in the bright sunlight. Her tension had eased somewhat, so that she didn't appear as rigid, and a few years had fallen off her face without that frown and pointy chin-lift thing.

"I'd love to stay and apologize for casting aspersions on your character. But I do need to get to my interview."

He nodded. "I understand. Just move your car. Fast."

"Done." She turned to walk back to her car, pausing once to glance back at him. "Thanks."

"You're welcome." Then, a spontaneous urge made him add, "Maybe I'll see you when you're finished."

She stopped and turned around, looking...interested.

Interesting.

"You'll be working all afternoon?"

He gestured toward the shop. "Lately it seems like I never get out of here. Some of these officers can man a billion-dollar nuclear submarine but don't know how to drain the transmission fluid out of a Chevy."

She nodded once, slowly. "Okay then. Maybe I'll see you."

If he had his way, she most definitely would. In fact, he might just have to make sure of it. Though it didn't need it, maybe he'd pop the hood on his much-babied '67 Impala and give her another oil change. A lengthy one.

He wanted to see this woman again. He didn't know her name—God, how could he not have gotten her name?—but he definitely wanted to learn it.

As she got in the car, he almost yelled to ask what he should call her if they happened to bump into each other again. But it seemed a little too pushy. If he was meant to know it, he'd know it. If he was meant to see her again, he'd see her again…oil change or no oil change.

Danny was a big believer in fate. That John Cusack movie, *Serendipity,* was a major chick flick and he'd pretended to gag his way through it when his sister had made him watch it once. But deep down, he kind of liked the idea.

He wasn't a very spiritual guy, but he did believe in things like karma and putting out good thoughts and getting them back in return. What goes around, comes around, that kind of stuff. Call it fate, or destiny, whatever.

Things happened for a reason. People came in and out of your life because they were meant to. And if the beautiful blonde was meant to come back into his, she would.

He stood by the motor pool, watching as she got into her little sedan, prepared to wave as she drove by. But a minute went by, and then another, and she didn't move.

It appeared she wasn't leaving his life quite as quickly as he'd thought.

Her door opened. One beautiful leg appeared, then she stepped out and turned to face him.

"My car won't start."

Danny lifted his eyes toward the sky and smiled. *Serendipity.*

2

Saturday, 5/7/11, 02:40 p.m.
www.mad-mari.com/2011/05/07/quickone
Just checking in between interviews on my phone.
I was so busy last night getting ready for 2day that I
forgot to put up my usual "Saturday Sinners" post.

Newbies—every Sat I talk about somebody who
has been very bad this week. Last Sat was about that
jerk whose wife found a YouTube vid of him marrying
another woman...without getting a divorce first.
"Sunday Saints" is about someone very good.

I guess I'm the sinner today 'cause I forgot to
blog. ;-)

Anyway, how about you guys take the floor? Say
h'lo to each other. I'll check in when I get home.
L8er—
Mari

MARISSA WAS HALFWAY THROUGH her meeting with a
woman from Human Resources, feeling confident she'd
rocked the interview with the Deputy to the Commandant, when she remembered her underpants.

Oh, not that she wasn't wearing them. That was impossible to forget. She'd picked a hell of a first time to go commando.

No, she didn't have to worry about panty lines, but there were definitely other distractions. Like getting used to, uh, *everything* being exposed to any random updraft.

So, no, she hadn't forgotten for one minute that she was pantyless beneath her skirt. But she had forgotten—however briefly—what she'd done with those panties. When the woman interviewing her made a comment about a white-glove ceremony, it popped into her mind that she'd left her silky black undergarment, along with her pantyhose, in her car's glove box.

And an adorably sexy, very nice mechanic was right now working on her car, having insisted he didn't mind trying to find out what was wrong with it while she was at her interview.

And in order to check out what was wrong with the car, he might need to get the owner's manual.

And while reaching into that glove box for that manual, he might just grab a fistful of recently worn lingerie.

Oh, God.

Under normal circumstances, a superhot, sexy dude touching her underwear might give her a little thrill. Normal circumstances being if said underwear happened to be on her person at the time.

But superhot, sexy dude finding them balled up in her car, and wondering what the hell kind of psycho takes off her underwear right before an important job interview?

Uh, yeah. Not so much.

"You are so screwed," she muttered with a groan.

"I'm sorry, what did you say?" asked the woman.

Things just go from bad to worse.

Fortunately, her interviewer was distracted, flipping through a file, and had barely glanced up. Yanking her thoughts together, Marissa stammered, "Uh, you're so… shrewd. I mean, the way you have everything organized." Forcing a laugh, she added, "My home office is a mess, I can never find anything."

"I see."

The woman offered her a tight smile. It could have been genuine, or it could have been her way of humoring Mari while she figured out a way to make sure the crazy blonde who talked to herself in the middle of a meeting didn't get hired. The woman probably already disliked her because she had to work on a Saturday, the Deputy to the Commandant being too busy with end-of-the-year activities to schedule a weekday interview.

Sighing deeply, Mari said, "Forgive me, I'm a little nervous. I'm mumbling."

The woman's face softened. "It's okay." Lowering her voice and leaning closer, she added, "And don't worry— you're not screwed. In fact, I think you did very well."

Oh, Lord. Definitely bad to worse. "I'm *so* sorry!"

"Don't worry about it. Believe me, I work around a bunch of sailors all the time. The language can be… salty."

The ice broken, they spent the next half hour talking about the job, which Marissa wanted more than ever. At first, it had just been about employment—getting paid to do something other than peddling overpriced shoes at a Harbor Place boutique so she could pay the bills. Now that she'd come here and learned more about the guest lecturer position—what she'd be doing, who she'd be talking to, why she was needed—she knew she wanted it. Badly.

As someone who'd had to play mom for her younger siblings from the age of fourteen, Marissa knew she was good with teens and young adults. She could relate to them—maybe because she'd still been a kid herself when she'd been thrust into such an adult role.

She could manage both mindsets. Could dish with her eighteen-year-old sister about some hot guy she'd met in Bio 101, but also put on the cautionary Mom hat and remind her that college was about learning, not about guys.

She could support her twenty-one-year-old brother when he decided to go to art school rather than finish college, and also worry about how he was going to support himself drawing comic books.

And as for her twenty-six-year-old brother, well, hers would be the shoulder he would lean on when he finally decided to come out to their incredibly old-fashioned, rigid father...who *so* wasn't equipped to deal with having a gay son.

Yes, she was definitely part old soul, part young adult, and had been for fifteen years. So she had the right background to deal with college kids.

Plus, she'd grown up in the military. She'd been a victim of one of its most common negative side effects—spouses unable to deal with it, families wrecked because of it. Kids raised by distant, rigid, militaristic parents. She knew what happened to the children of weak mothers who couldn't cope and cheating fathers who couldn't love.

"The Deputy to the Commandant told you why some midshipmen will be returning here before the official start of the summer semester?" asked the interviewer.

Mari nodded. "He said they are faced with washing out."

"Yes. Some should, either for academic reasons or lack of seriousness about their decision to attend."

"I'm sure there are some who apply for the wrong reasons."

"Exactly. Others, though, might succeed, but they're unsure about whether they can live a military life, or have unrealistic expectations about what that life entails."

"Hence the need for a reality check."

"Exactly."

Bringing in guests to talk to these young men and women on their own terms, about real-life issues they faced—outside the day-to-day of the military—seemed like a very good idea. One guest speaker was an accountant who would be showing them what their financial futures might look like. Another was a diplomat who'd be talking about the big world picture.

And if she got the job, Mari—Dr. Marissa Marshall, who wrote a dissertation on the effect of the military on relationships and families—would be discussing their personal lives. Dating, marriage, children. Confusion over gender roles and the trouble sexism can bring into a household. The costs, the sacrifices, the potential pitfalls.

It made sense. A lot of sense. She only hoped the deputy agreed she was the right person for the job, and that he wasn't too worried about her age, which he'd mentioned a couple of times during their meeting.

After a few more minutes of conversation, Marissa finished in Personnel and headed out of the building, toward the parking lot. Her thoughts were in a jumble. Images of a good job—doing good things for students in need of support—mixed with the picture of a stranger with her underwear in his hand.

His big, strong, powerful hand. Hmm.

But when she arrived at the parking lot, seeing the empty spot where her car had been parked, she began to imagine another scenario. Her, on the phone, reporting her car stolen.

Because it wasn't in the parking lot.

God, had she really been so flustered, so worried about the time and her stupid freaking underwear, that she'd handed over her keys to a complete stranger? Where on earth was the smart, sensible Marissa, or even the suspicions, skeptical Mari?

"Hey, there, how'd it go?"

Relief washed over her as she heard a voice calling from the open bay of the garage building. The handsome Midas man emerged from the shadowy interior, still dressed in his mechanic's coveralls.

"Pretty well," she admitted, approaching him slowly. Then, not about to ask if he'd looked in the glove box, she added, "I guess you were able to get my car started?"

He jerked a thumb over his shoulder, pointing into the shadowy recesses of the garage. "Jumped it and drove it in here so I could work on it. Not a big deal, your battery was dead as a doornail. I ran out and picked one up and popped it in."

Eyes widening, she replied, "Seriously?"

"Yep. I also changed the oil while I was at it." He shook his head in disapproval. "Speaking of which, you do know motor oil's supposed to be a liquid, right? The stuff that came outta there was the color and the consistency of tar. When's the last time you had it changed?"

She'd been meaning to do that for a good year. Or two.

"I guess I forgot. Sorry."

"Don't tell me, tell her."

She lifted a confused brow. "Her?"

He gestured toward her car again. "She'll get even with you if you neglect her. Why do you think she was rattling like a bag of bones?"

He sounded like he was talking about a loved one. "I take it you like cars."

"They do call me the Midas man," he said, tapping the letters stitched on his chest.

"Yeah, I noticed."

"But to answer your question, I sort of like cars. Maybe about as much as Winnie-the-Pooh likes honey."

The very idea of this big, rugged man knowing who Winnie-the-Pooh was made her chuckle. And the fact that he'd actually admitted it? Even more noteworthy. Most guys would be too worried about being considered wusses to dare say such a thing.

"Fortunately, cars can be obtained without having to climb trees or fight off bees," she countered.

"What's the matter," he asked with a grin, "your grocery store doesn't carry Sue-Bee?"

She chuckled again, liking him more with every passing minute. She liked his wit, liked his smile. Adored those dimples. "So, how much do I owe you?" she asked, shaking off the mental lapse into la-la-lust land.

"Not much," he told her, naming a figure.

He was right. It wasn't much. In fact, it sounded far too low for an auto repair. "Wait, that's just for the parts. What about the labor charges?"

He waved a hand. "It was a twenty-minute job. Piece of cake."

"I couldn't…"

"Sure you could. Let's call it Be Kind To Others Day."

What a nice sentiment, especially coming from such a strong, young man. He had surprised her again, revealing a depth of warmth and kindness she didn't usually encounter in men she met. It seemed out-of-place with his raw, masculine good looks and his career.

"The next time you have the chance to do a simple, twenty-minute favor to help out a stranger, go for it and think of me," he added.

Uh, interesting way to put it. Going for *it* while thinking of him…that might not be very difficult. But there they were again, back to quibbling about those *its*.

She could do as he asked—pay it forward—and she would. But she had another idea, too. She cast a quick look at the ring finger on his left hand, not seeing a band of gold. Though a mechanic might take a wedding ring off when working, she didn't see any distinctive tan line, either. So she hoped she was right in deducing he wasn't married. Whether he was unattached, she couldn't know. But it was worth finding out.

Mari hadn't been out with a man in a long time. It had been even longer since she'd actually been the one to ask for a date.

It's not a date. It's a thank-you.

Right. It was the least she could do. What anyone would do.

Would you do it if he was seventy, with a long, greasy gray ponytail, a hairy back and tattoos?

She told that little voice in her head to shut the hell up, then took a deep breath. Hoping she hadn't misread interest when he was just being a nice guy who treated every woman like she was something special, she said,

"You've got a deal. But can I also buy you a late lunch or an early dinner as a thank-you?"

She held herself rigid, waiting for his answer.

"You don't have to do that."

Not exactly a refusal. But not a yes, either.

"Here's another idea," he said. "How about you spring for a couple of burgers and come with me to the marina? We can take my boat out and watch the sunset over the water."

Oh, wow. That definitely sounded more like a date than a thank-you. A very intimate, romantic kind of date, which was crazy since she didn't even know this guy.

Don't be stupid. Women go on blind dates all the time with men they've never met.

But in a boat, far from land? How crazy was that? What if he turned out to be some Freddy Krueger type? Her plastic-wrapped body parts might wash ashore all up and down the eastern seaboard. What if they never found her head?

He held up a hand, palm out. "Wait, scratch that. You don't even know me—I shouldn't have put you on the spot. You're probably worrying I'm going to kidnap you or something."

Or something.

She didn't say anything. Not a word. Especially not about her fear that they wouldn't find her head.

"But lunch would be great, thanks. I'm glad you asked."

"You wanted me to?"

"If you hadn't, I would have. Believe me, I wasn't going to let you leave without at least getting your name."

"It's Mari...Marissa." She extended her hand in greeting.

"Mari," he said, zoning in on her nickname, as though he'd immediately decided it suited her better than her formal one. It was like he could see past the rigid hair-style and the plain clothes and the reason she was here and already knew the more free-spirited woman who lay beneath all that. "Nice to meet you, Mari. I'm Danny."

He took her hand in his larger one, and she forgot to breathe for a second, wondering why such a simple touch made her shiver. His skin was warm, his grip firm, the fingers strong and the palm rough. And he didn't let go right away, hesitating for the briefest moment, as if he, too, were savoring the first connection of skin-on-skin.

Their stares met. He'd pushed his sunglasses onto the top of his head and the late afternoon sunshine brought a brilliant gleam to those amber eyes. The gentle smile of pleasure on his face told her so many things—that he was glad to have met her, that he had wanted to ask her out, that he did look forward to getting to know her.

That he was interested. Maybe even as interested as she was. And she, being totally honest with herself, was *very* interested. More interested in him than she'd been in any man for a very long time.

They might have nothing in common, might not know each other, but they definitely had sparks. Electricity. Plus he was kind, thoughtful…and sexy as hell. Anyone with a fully functioning vagina would be interested.

Finally releasing her hand, he said, "Can I admit I was grateful for your dead battery?"

"Really?"

"Yeah. It saved me from having to dump a box of nails in the parking lot, hoping you'd run over them and flatten a tire, so I'd have to help you out."

She laughed softly, liking that he'd been so serious

about seeing her again…even if his methods sounded a little outrageous. Then again, it wasn't like he'd acted on them.

"Mental note. Potential stalker," she said, her tone wry.

"I just know a good thing when I see it." He lowered his voice to add, "You're somebody I want to get to know better."

"Why? Because I'm nervy enough to park illegally at a naval academy?"

"Well, yeah," he said, his mouth quirking higher on one side. That twinkle reappeared and he seemed wickedly amused as he added, "Plus, I just have to know more about a girl who takes off her underwear and leaves them in her car right before a big job interview."

DANNY PROBABLY SHOULDN'T have said anything about finding Mari's undergarments in her glove compartment. He'd caught her off guard, and the gentleman he'd claimed to be definitely wouldn't have brought it up. He could easily have pretended he had never seen a thing, saving both of them from embarrassment.

But Danny was ungentlemanly enough that he couldn't help it. Mari was just too sexy to resist, and too contradictory not to try to figure out.

He couldn't deny he'd been very curious about her even before he'd found the wadded-up ball of fabric in her car. And once he had? Whoa. Reaching in for the manual to check the engine specs and winding up with his hand covered in soft, silky, woman-scented material had been a delightful shock. He'd already been sure he wanted to get to know her better. That surprising discovery had changed the very meaning of the word *know* to a much more carnal variation.

It hadn't taken a lot of imagination to put everything together and figure out what she'd done. There'd been their previous conversation, her nervousness, the way she'd been fiddling around in her car when he'd first come out to warn her away from the Employees Only parking lot.

He had to admit, he hadn't been sure how she would react when he told her she'd been busted. But she hadn't slapped his face or stalked away or cussed him out.

She'd groaned once. Her pretty face had turned a little bit pink. Then she'd burst into laughter, as if she couldn't hold it in anymore. Even now, several seconds later, unrestrained giggles erupted from her lips as she tried to explain.

"You…aren't supposed to know that!"

He wagged his eyebrows. "I didn't, not 100%. Not until you just confirmed it, anyway."

She slapped her palm against her forehead. "I can't believe I fell for it. I should have pretended I had no idea what you were talking about."

"That *might* have worked, but, uh, I was pretty sure. Now, fess up…is that what we were really talking about earlier?"

"'Fraid so."

Remembering everything he'd said before, he added, "So you thought I was offering to get in your car and, what, give you *directions* on how to pull up your own underwear?"

"Something like that."

He snorted. "The day I need to use a line like that is the day I trade in my single-man-on-the-prowl club card."

Her smile might have faded the tiniest bit. "Are you?"

"Am I what? Single?"

"And on the prowl?"

Knowing she was questioning her own instincts, wondering if he was some kind of sleazy on-the-make playboy, he answered her truthfully. "Yes and no. I'm single, but I haven't been accused of prowling since I was ten and played my last game of Ding-Dong-Dash at old Mrs. McCurdy's house."

"Ding-Dong…"

"You know. Ring the doorbell and run? Didn't you ever play that as a kid?"

She shuddered. "I grew up on military bases. No doorbells. And not much of a sense of humor from most of the guys who lived behind those doors."

"Yeah, well, old Mrs. McCurdy didn't laugh much, either."

One corner of her mouth went up. "You got caught?"

"Uh-huh. She was pretty spry for being on the verge of mummification."

Tsking, she shook her head. "Couldn't outrun an old lady. Bet your friends didn't let you live that one down."

"Nope, even though they all bailed on me when she grabbed me by the back of the shirt and dragged me into the house so she could call my parents."

"Uh-oh. Sounds like the opening of a horror movie on the Chiller channel."

"Just about. Get this, while we waited for my folks to show up, she made me look at her poor, swollen feet to show me how horrible I'd been to make her get up to answer the door."

"Eww!"

"Tell me about it. Old lady feet—is there anything worse to a ten-year-old boy?"

"Bet you never rang any doorbells and ran again," she quipped.

He held his fingers up in a Scout's promise. "Not once."

"She sounds like a smart old lady."

His lips quirked. "She was. I felt so guilty afterward I always brought her paper up onto her porch instead of tossing it into the driveway." Then he added, "And she definitely taught me a lesson."

"About ringing doorbells?"

"About feet. If you ever need something to kill a fleeting moment of happiness, or a glimmer of sexual interest? Just think of old feet."

"Noted. But for the record, I happen to have great feet and I don't intend to let that change." Her smile was bright and comfortable, as if she'd finally let down all guard, and was being completely herself for the first time since they'd met.

"Great feet, huh? Most people wouldn't claim that."

She shrugged. "Don't ask what I think about my goofy-looking ears or my thin, flat hair, but I have supreme confidence in my feet. Even pedicurists compliment them."

He glanced down at the sexy, spike-heeled pumps. He'd like to pull them off and closely examine those feet. Then work his way up. Inch by devastating inch.

He already knew he'd have to add her calves to the list of fabulous body parts. And he suspected if he kept going up those legs, he'd find quite a few more.

Danny shook his head, hard. Jesus, this woman was turning him into some kind of hound dog. He never started immediately thinking about how sexy a woman was right after meeting her. If she was attractive? Sure.

Smart? Yeah. But downright I-think-I'll-die-if-I-can't-go-to-bed-with-you-soon thoughts? Uh-uh.

He knew why. It wasn't just how attractive she was—he'd met plenty of attractive women. It was because of the sharp bolt of utter, mouth-watering want that had roared through him when he'd stuck his hand in her glove compartment and found himself wrist-deep in sexy, feminine undergarments. The flood of images that had gone through his brain, the sweet scent lingering in the air, the silky feel against his skin. All that had combined to put him on red alert.

Even changing her car's battery and checking her oil had done nothing to cool him down. Because he'd thought about nothing but charging *her* battery and slickening up *her* engine.

"I might not ever be in line to model Dior in Paris, but I bet I could sell a lot of Dr. Scholl's at Target. So you might just be in luck when it comes to *my* old lady feet," she said with a laugh. "I might even be able to pull off flip-flops at seventy and not make you want to hurl."

Her words brought an image to his mind—him still knowing her, all those years in the future. And for some reason, Danny didn't laugh with her.

Maybe it was that crazy karma thing—fate, serendipity. Whatever the reason, despite being a thirty-three-year-old bachelor, he suddenly found the idea of being with someone for *that* long, knowing someone *that* intimately, a little appealing.

Oh, it had always appealed to him when he thought of his parents and grandparents, all of whom were alive and happy back in Chicago. But he hadn't really given much thought to it for himself. He'd been focused on so many other things.

First, of course, on flight. That he'd focused on from

the age of five when his mechanic father had first taken him to a field beneath a landing flight path at O'Hare and he'd felt the power of a 747 shaking his small body like an earthquake.

Then, during a family trip to Disney World, he'd gotten his dad to take him over to Kennedy to watch a shuttle launch. And he'd suddenly begun to dream about another kind of flight altogether.

Everything he'd done since that point had been with an eye toward space.

He knew it would take years—and he'd planned his route carefully, knowing how most astronauts made their way into the manned space flight program. He'd listed his goals—air flight, navy, NASA—and pursued them with diligence from the time he hit high school, making sure he got the grades to get into Annapolis. Succeeding at this very academy had been key. Not just for everything that would come later, but also to justify the expense and sacrifices his family had made to get him here.

Then, on to the navy. He'd finished at the Academy, gone to Pensacola, then to Whiting.

Then to Afghanistan.

And there, everything had sort of fallen apart.

Not anymore. Now he was back on track. Back on schedule.

So why the hell was he suddenly thinking about what it might be like to grow old with someone, when his focus should be entirely on awaiting word on his application to the Astronaut Candidate Training Program?

"Anyway, back to my little wardrobe malfunction," she said, apparently not having noticed his distraction. "I had a run in my hose, and…"

"You panicked."

"Exactly."

Part of him was tempted to ask her if she'd had a run in her sexy black panties, too, but he figured that might be pushing his luck.

Besides, he didn't want to think about her sexy black panties any more than he had to. He especially didn't want to think about the fact that she wasn't wearing them right now. That just wasn't good for his sanity.

But it was tough to turn off the mental images, knowing she wasn't wearing a thing beneath that sinfully tight skirt. Under that simple black fabric was soft skin, curves and hollows and everything deliciously female.

You're an officer and a gentleman. An officer and a gentleman.

"So I made a spur-of-the-moment decision."

"Sure, I get that," he said, pulling his mind out of his own pants. "I mean, I once spilled tomato juice on my dress whites and had to go on duty in my skivvies."

She rolled her eyes. "Ha-ha."

"Look at it this way—I bet your, uh, state of undress provided a distraction from the interview, so maybe it made you a little less nervous."

"Are you kidding? I remembered they were in the glove box halfway through my second meeting, and immediately panicked, thinking you might find them."

"Well, I did," he admitted. "But trust me, I'm not some perv. They're not hanging from my rearview mirror or anything. I put them right back where I found them. In case you, uh…have need of them."

"Believe me, I usually do." She sighed heavily. "I know you won't get this—no guy would—but I just couldn't deal with a bunch of he-man jerks staring at my butt today."

He'd been staring at her butt today. But he didn't think

it wise to point that out. And he wasn't a he-man. Plus, he wasn't entirely sure what going bare-ass naked beneath her skirt had to do with it. Men stared. Period.

"And panty lines would have just begged to be stared at," she continued, quickly explaining her thinking on the whole nylons-smoothing-things-out theory.

Which, frankly, was just bullshit. Men definitely didn't need panty lines acting as little arrows to guide the eye to the perfect female posterior. Maybe other chicks would notice and care. If he did see them, a guy wouldn't be thinking about anything except pulling those elastic panty lines down. Preferably with his teeth.

"I'm afraid ass-appreciation is just part of our genetic code," he admitted. "Like flicking other naked guys with towels in the locker room, and our inability to ask for directions when we're lost."

"Yeah, what's with that?"

He shrugged. "It's a mystery."

"And one I'm not sure I want to solve."

"Some things you're better off not knowing."

"Like men shouldn't really want to understand why women go to the bathroom together?"

He leaned closer, lowering his voice conspiratorially. "It's all prearranged, right? So you can compare notes on the guys you're with, and escape together out the window if they suck, right?"

"Busted."

Nodding, he said, "So I guess that means you're in trouble today, since you're flying without a wingman when we go out for lunch."

She smiled up at him, her eyes gleaming in anticipation. "You mean on your boat?"

Growing still, Danny eyed her steadily, liking the

idea, but also knowing she'd hesitated earlier because she'd been unsure. "We don't have to."

She glanced outside at the beautiful late afternoon sky. "I'd love to." Then she looked down at herself and sighed. "But unfortunately, I'm not exactly dressed for it. My only spare clothes are, well, you know…"

Yeah. He knew. Her spare clothes were in her glove compartment and just the thought of her in nothing but them was enough to send an extra pint of blood toward his cock. Of course, knowing she was currently without them was doing a damn fine job of that already.

"How about this," he said, "it's only three-thirty, hours until sunset. You go to the nearest store and grab a cheap pair of jeans, I'll go take a shower. We can meet again at that Irish pub on West Street in exactly forty-five minutes. We'll get to know each other. Then, if you'd like, we'll go to the marina and take the boat out for a little while."

She nibbled her bottom lip between her teeth. "You're sure? I mean, you didn't rescind your invitation earlier because you'd changed your mind and don't want to, right? Did I back you into a corner on this?"

He held his arms up, gesturing to the wide-open space of the garage bay that surrounded them. "No corners. No arm-twisting." Then, stepping closer—close enough that his boot-covered feet nearly touched the pointy tips of her sexy shoes, hiding what were rumored to be magnificent feet, he added, "Let's just go for it and see what happens, okay?"

"There's that *it* again," she mumbled.

"What?"

Shaking her head, she stared up at him, those big blue eyes softening. Her lips parted and she drew a slow, audible breath over them, as if she realized he was talking about going for a lot more than lunch.

He didn't mean sex. At least, not right away. What he wanted to go for was a chance. Just an opportunity.

They'd clicked on sight. Now he wanted to know if that click could ignite something even more than a spark of sexual attraction.

A kiss would be a good start. One slow, deep, wet kiss, just to see what happened.

He wanted that—at least that—before this day was out. And if the kiss was as good as he suspected it could be, well, then they'd just have to see what happened.

"Okay," she finally said. "I think we've got a date."

$\underline{3}$

Saturday, 5/7/10, 03:45 p.m.
www.mad-mari.com/2011/05/07/quickone
Comment #21

Mari here, checking in again. Yay for the iPhone!

Glad you're chatting w/out me. Yeah, I agree with all of you that the businessman from last Sat was not only a scum-bucket for committing bigamy, but was also trés stupid to let somebody videotape his crime. And Jan from Chicago—lol on, "Would rather see the video of wife #1 beating the crap out of him when she found out." You & me both, sister!

Can't stay longer; there've been some interesting developments today. Real quick, tho, let me just say, the interviews went great. I think I might actually get the gig.

And after the interview, something else happened. Something…surprising. Remember that sea of testosterone I said I was diving into? Well, I think I have come face-to-face with the great white.
Let's hope he doesn't eat me up. ;-)

Bye!

MARI HAD NO TROUBLE FINDING the small, downtown pub, which Danny said had an outside patio on which they could enjoy the warmth of the afternoon. And true to his word, he showed up exactly forty-five minutes later, his golden-brown hair still damp from his shower and his face clean-shaven. Marissa saw him arrive, and had to stand in the restaurant vestibule, watching him out the front window for a few moments. Because, oh, God, was he nice to look at.

She'd known he was good-looking, had recognized that immediately. But he cleaned up utterly gorgeous. Traffic-stoppingly, heart-poundingly, panty-dampeningly—and she was wearing panties now—gorgeous.

Then there was the body. Wow.

That deserved a repeat: Wow.

Wearing jeans and a T-shirt, without the loose-fitting work clothes covering him up from neck to ankle, his entire rock-hard form was on perfect masculine display. And mercy, could the man do things for some Levi's and oh, did his shoulders ever stretch out endlessly under that gray cotton.

Aside from the broad shoulders, he was also lean-waisted, slim-hipped, long-legged. Built like he'd been molded out of clay by an artist trying to depict the perfect male form.

Why in the name of God is he going out with you?

She wasn't being overly modest or highly critical of her own appeal. In fact, Marissa knew she was somewhat attractive.

Not beautiful, by any means. Not with her funky ears and her too-thin hair—which looked particularly lank now that she'd taken it out of that bun and left it hanging loose. Then there was the hint of a belly she could never totally flatten, no matter how many death-by-sit-up sessions she endured at the gym.

She'd cop to nice-looking, maybe a little sexy—she did have good legs and perky boobs that didn't even need a Wonderbra—but she wasn't drop-dead stunning. She might turn a few heads but no way would she ever cause gawking guys to step into traffic or obsessed secret admirers to send sky-banners into the air proclaiming her hotness.

So why on earth would this hunky guy want to be with her? Unless, of course, he'd been telling the truth— that he just wanted to get to know the girl who'd ditched her underwear.

That spoke of someone with a sense of humor. Someone who was interested in more than just physical appearance, and actually cared about personality. Someone she could like. A lot.

But oh, did she ever hope there was some lust there, too.

"Hi, see you found it," he said as he entered the Irish restaurant he'd sent her to, a cute place that was more trendy than publike. He smelled clean and fresh and spicy, his subtle aftershave making her think of all good things male. "And I see you found something else to wear?"

She glanced down at her new clothes. In popular Annapolis, it hadn't taken her more than a half hour to find a shop and grab a pair of casual pants and a lightweight sweater, and not break her bank doing it. She'd changed into the outfit in the restaurant's ladies' room. She'd put her underwear back on, too. The pants fit fine…no panty lines.

"Yes, I did."

His gaze zoned in on her hair, the ash-blond tresses

hanging down over her shoulders like a veil. His voice a hint lower, thicker, he said, "Don't ever wear that hideous bun again, okay?"

She swallowed, feeling her legs tremble the tiniest bit under the full onslaught of his close-up, admiring attention. "It was supposed to make me look older, more mature around students."

"Trust me on this, they're going to be busy enough staring at your...panty lines."

Oh, joy.

"They're not going to be distracted by any old-lady hairstyle." He lifted a hand, running his fingers through a long strand, as if savoring the texture. "Besides, it's beautiful."

Okay, it was soft. Thin, but soft. And, all right, the color was pretty. At least, this man's rapt attention made her think so. She managed a shaky smile and swallowed hard, willing her heartbeat to slow down. It was just that the simple brush of those fingertips on her hair, the faint scrape of his thumb on her cheek had been so incredibly nice. Which made her wonder what a *real* touch might be like.

Earth-shattering.

Well, a few of them in a row almost certainly would be.

Another couple walked in the door, reminding them that they were blocking it. Taking her elbow, he smiled politely and led her to the empty hostess station. Then, glancing down at her feet, he murmured, "I see you didn't hit a shoe store. Those aren't exactly seaworthy."

No, they weren't. The pointy pumps might be a little dressy for her outfit. But they were also sexy, and the man liked them. She'd seen that in his eyes when they'd had that silly conversation about her feet. "I guess not," she conceded.

"Does that mean you've already made up your mind about the sunset? Not gonna trust me?"

"Well, you didn't steal my car," she said.

"That's me. Not a car thief."

"And you showed up when you said you would. You didn't stand me up."

"Not a jerk, either."

She smiled up at him. "I think I can trust you."

"Good," he said, a warmth in his stare loading that simple word with additional meaning. He was glad and was looking forward to spending more time with her.

Mari tingled a little, feeling her skin pucker as she thought about lying on the deck of a boat with him. It definitely wasn't bikini weather, but she suspected he could keep her warm without much effort.

A hostess approached, her gaze immediately zeroing in on Danny. Big surprise. Stepping the tiniest bit closer to her date, Marissa said, "I figured if we do go for a sunset cruise, I'd probably want to take them off and get my feet wet, anyway."

Apparently not even noticing the other woman's overly-warm-for-a-hostess-smile, he tsked. "And risk damaging perfection with unforgiving saltwater?"

"You have a thing for feet?" the hostess asked with a little simper.

"Not old ones," Marissa replied.

That had come out of her mouth purely by reflex because of the conversation they'd had earlier. It had not been meant as a snotty comment to the hostess, who was probably close to forty.

But the woman still stiffened, her smile growing tight.

As they followed her in silence, she felt Danny's broad shoulders moving in silent amusement.

They took their seats, watched the woman walk away, then Danny muttered, "Meow."

Shaking her head, genuinely embarrassed, she said, "I didn't mean…"

He held a hand up. "I'm kidding. I know you were talking about our earlier conversation. Just yanking your chain."

His mischievous expression brought a smile to her lips—the same smile she'd had on her face almost every minute since she'd met him. Well, at least the minutes since he'd admitted he'd found her underwear in her car, and had been amused by it.

She kept smiling as they glanced at the menus. Chuckling as they sipped their drinks. Laughing as they ate their lunch and playfully argued over whether Christian Bale or Michael Keaton had been the better Batman. That was followed by a dozen other get-to-know-you bits of nonsense that didn't matter but were vitally important just the same.

Important because every word he said, no matter how innocuous, was uttered in that husky male voice and accompanied by that devastatingly attractive smile. And deep down she knew that every damn one of them was a replacement for the conversation they were having in their own minds. Their layer of small talk was a veneer, a thin coating covering up the questions they weren't asking.

Do you feel it? Am I alone in this? Are we crazy?

With every word, every laugh, every shared glance, every brush of their hands on the table or glance of each other's mouths, hands, bodies, the heat grew. She knew it by the way his hand lingered when he reached over to pull a wind-blown leaf out of her hair. By the way he shifted in his chair, sliding his foot closer, until their legs brushed under the table. And when he took a plump cherry tomato out of his salad and held it to her lips, it took all her strength of will not to flick her tongue out and take some salt off his skin to flavor it.

They had come here just to "see what happened." She had no doubt that what had happened was that the chemistry and physical attraction between them had grown so thick she could almost bite into it. By the time they'd finished eating and called for the check, she was ready to lean over the table, grab two fistfuls of his thick hair and drag him in for a hot, wet kiss.

Crazy. He's a stranger!

Well, not really. Their conversation hadn't revealed a whole lot. Not even, she realized, their last names. But she knew he was the oldest child from a big family—like her. Knew he had read the latest bestsellers but couldn't stand Oprah books. Knew he had a '67 Impala that he treated like a golden carriage. Knew he flexed his right hand once in a while, as if he had an ache in it. Knew he picked the tomatoes out of his salad.

She knew she wanted him. That was the most important thing, the only thing that really mattered to her right now.

Being totally honest, not only was she comfortable going on this man's boat with him—or just about anywhere else he asked—but she also hoped she'd still be on it tomorrow morning. A quick call to a neighbor who sometimes looked after Brionne, her cat, and she'd be all set. She was probably being totally Mad-Mari about this, but she wanted to have sex with him. Tonight.

Mari had never been the type to have one-night stands, though she'd had one or two affairs that didn't last much

longer than a week. But somehow, even if she was told
that there was no way she would ever see Danny again,
she wouldn't care. She wanted a night in his arms. In his
bed. Wanted his hands and his mouth and every inch of
his skin touching hers. Right or wrong, the past or the
future didn't have anything to do with it. She just *wanted*.
Now.

Besides, if she was really about to dive into her
real life—everything she'd been planning for all these
years—wasn't one last fling in order? Why not have one
last Mad-Mari romp with a hot, sexy, blue collar guy
who she couldn't envision in her future?

Not the past. Not the future. Just the present.

And he would be a present—to *her*—of that she had
no doubt.

"So," he said as he polished off the last of his fries,
"you ever been married?"

She shook her head. "You?"

"Just to my job."

"It's really important to you?" she asked, a little surprised. Yes, he appeared to love cars, especially his own,
but he seemed so damned smart and capable. Was there
really nothing else he could be doing with his life?

"It's the only thing I've ever wanted. I have ever since
I was five years old and my dad took me with him to
work at O'Hare one day."

"What did he do?"

"He was a lead mechanic for an airline, until he re-
tired. So how about you? I gotta admit, I have a hard time
picturing you being old enough to teach college kids."

"I'm twenty-nine. Just got my doctorate in psychology
and I'm testing out the waters."

He gaped. "I don't know where to start. The doctorate
at twenty-nine part, or the fact that you're a shrink."

The reaction was a familiar one. Especially the psychologist part. Everybody worried about that one, as if she would be head-shrinking them from their first meeting.

"So, Doctor, I've been having this pain…"

"I'm not an M.D." She laughed. "I couldn't even prescribe you an aspirin."

"Still, I'd be using that 'Doctor' all over the place if I had the right to."

She couldn't prevent a tiny smile. Because, yeah, she did like hearing it once in a while. She'd sure worked hard enough to earn it. "My best friend says I kept going to school just to avoid having to be responsible for anything else."

"Else?"

Wishing she hadn't brought it up, she skimmed over her family history, not giving in to old habits by sharing what lousy parents she'd been born to. That was just too depressing. But she did have to mention the breakup… and, as lightly as she could, her mother's abandonment. What an upbeat first date she was!

"So, family responsibilities, school for almost a decade. No time for fun?" he asked, skimming over her past as if realizing she didn't want to say any more about it.

"Define *fun*."

"Dating?"

"I don't usually call dating fun."

"Oooh, that sounds pessimistic."

"Pragmatic. The last guy I dated couldn't handle being with a woman with my I.Q."

"You have a pretty high I.Q., huh?"

"Not especially, but *he* couldn't even spell it!" She waved away any more questions, rolling her eyes. "I was stupid and lonely, so I broke my own number one dating rule."

"Which is?"

"I never go out with soldiers."

"Smart thinking," he said with an exaggerated shudder. "So, how about sex?"

Sure. The word came to her tongue but didn't fall off it.

"That's fun," she slowly replied. "At least, if I'm remembering correctly."

His eyes darkened the tiniest bit, and his smile thinned, as if he regretted getting them into this intimate a conversation. But he didn't immediately back them out of it.

"Yeah, so I hear."

"Don't tell me *your* memory's fuzzy."

"Probably more so than you'd imagine."

Hmm.

"But from what I remember, oh, yeah, I'd call it fun. Especially when it lasts for hours and you aren't sure whether you're alive or dead because it doesn't seem possible that anything can feel so damn good," he said, his voice unwavering. But it wasn't throaty or seductive; he merely sounded very sure of what he was saying.

She breathed deeply, in and out, willing her heart to stop racing. Then she finally nodded. "Interesting," she murmured, hearing the weakness of her voice.

So interesting her thighs were locking together reflexively under the table. Good thing she'd put those panties back on. Otherwise she suspected the seam of her new slacks would be damp right now. Heaven knew her panties were.

"So should we talk about how much you can have

fun at theme parks now?" he asked, those amber eyes twinkling.

She slowly shook her head.

"What *do* you want to do?"

She could tell the truth, just throw it out there on the table and see how he responded. They were waltzing around the subject like a couple on *Dancing with the Stars*.

Besides, she'd already made the first move once today by asking him out. Why shouldn't she take another shot?

Because asking somebody to lunch is a little different than asking him to rock your world and give you many, many orgasms.

"Ahem." She cleared her throat, reaching for her water.

"Oh," he said knowingly.

She swallowed, then eyed him over the glass. "Oh, what?"

"Oh. Now we both have sex on the brain. I'm sorry, but I've been thinking about nothing else but kissing you for hours, I guess I should've stuck with that."

His voice was silky smooth, intimate. There was warmth in his eyes, but no humor. As if he, too, was ready to move past the light, friendly conversation they'd engaged in throughout lunch and get a whole lot more serious pretty damn quick.

"Kissing?" she murmured, fascinated by the idea.

He nodded once. Then, wordlessly, he leaned across the small table, touching his fingers to her chin to tilt her face up. The briefest of hesitations—to give her a chance to back away—then he moved his mouth to hers.

Mari's heart flipped in her chest, she was aware of that much. Then *nothing*, except the feel of his warm lips against hers, the warmth of his breath flavored with the sweetness and lemon he'd had in his iced tea. It was soft, tender maybe a little tentative as they both acknowledged the importance of this moment.

A first kiss was a critical thing. It set a tone, lifted a bar. Mari had walked away from good-looking men who didn't know how to kiss.

This man did. Oh, God, did he ever.

Not forcing her mouth open and thrusting his tongue down her throat, he instead nibbled lightly, seemed content with just the joining of their lips. A slow build. It was a quiet kiss…sexy in its very patience and innocence.

Frankly, it drove her crazy. Mari wanted more, so much more. Groaning, she parted her lips, sliding her tongue out to taste his, not giving a damn about where they were or who might see. She just needed more of him.

He gave her more, sliding his hand up to cup her cheek, tangling his fingers in her hair, tilting his head to deepen things. And then, he cooled down, going back to sweet and light, until he finally lifted his mouth from hers and pulled away.

She heard her choppy breaths, and his, and knew he had been every bit as affected.

It had been a good first kiss. A very good start to *whatever* this was. "I want to go on your boat with you," she admitted. "To…see the sunset."

"We *can* just watch the sunset," he said, his voice low and tight, as if the idea pained him. "No other expectations."

"I know." Then, emboldened by the need still swirling through her after that kiss, she added, "Or we can kiss again."

He smiled. "That sounds like…fun."

Remembering what they'd been saying before that kiss—about how to have fun—she smiled back. "Yes, it does."

Their stares met and held, both of them knowing what they were really talking about. "You're sure?"

"Uh-huh. So sure I don't even mind too much if you think I'm easy."

He reached across the table, taking her hand, squeezing lightly. "I don't. Because, for the record, I'm feeling exactly the same way and I know I'm not easy."

That pleased her. She hoped what was happening between them was as unique for him as it was for her.

"Okay then. Let's get outta here." He reached into his pocket for his wallet.

She immediately shook her head. "Not only am I not easy, I'm not a welcher. It's on me, remember?"

Ooh. Shouldn't have thought about anything being on her. Because that made her think of all the other things she'd like on her. Well, one other thing. Him.

"Thank you," he said simply.

She liked that he didn't make an issue of it. She would have been disappointed if he'd gotten all he-man instead of letting her do what she'd wanted to do—repay him for helping her with her car.

It simply reinforced what she already suspected about Danny. He was extremely confident in his own masculinity, not the type to feel threatened by something like a woman making the first move or buying him a cheeseburger.

Oh, how she liked him. And she suspected that, by the end of the night, she would like him a whole lot more.

4

Saturday, 5/7/10, 05:25 p.m.
www.mad-mari.com/2011/05/07/quickone
Comment #74

Okay, one last comment for the day, then I'm turning this phone off and not checking in again. Just wanted you all to know that tomorrow's Sunday Sinner post might be a little late.

I also might have a whole lot of inspiration for writing it.

At least, if I'm lucky. ;-)

See ya!

BEING IN THE NAVY, USED to being moved around and living all over the world, Danny had never bought a house of his own. He either lived on base, or sometimes off base in an apartment. He'd invested in only two things of substance—both of which were mobile. One was, of course, his classic car, which he, with the help of his dad and brothers, had spent a full year restoring.

The other was *Jazzie Girl*, his 27-foot cruiser, which he kept at one of the local marinas. Simple, yet graceful with her 40-foot mast, she was his escape clause when he wanted water instead of air. Flying was his first choice, always, but sometimes he just liked hoisting the sails and exploring the Chesapeake.

He saw by the look on Mari's face as they pulled into the marina that she liked the water. He had the feeling she would especially like it on a breezy afternoon like this one, when they'd skim over the bay like a stone skipped on a flat pond.

"These are beautiful," she said, staring from vessel to vessel, many of which were much larger—and far more grand—than his. The late afternoon sun sent gleams of gold over the beautifully curved structures which danced on the water. "I'm so excited, I've never been sailing."

Surprised, he asked, "Seriously? Where do you live?" It was something they hadn't even gotten around to discussing. God did he hoped she didn't say Kansas or Buffalo or anywhere far away.

"Near the harbor in Baltimore," she admitted with a self-deprecating shrug, obviously realizing this entire area was a boating mecca. "I've just never known anyone who had a boat. Remember, I was an army brat, not a navy one."

"Well, let's find out if you have sea legs. There she is," he said, pointing toward his slip.

They walked closer and she murmured, *"Jazzie Girl?"*

He groaned a little. "My sister harassed me into it. She said since I didn't name my firstborn after her, she should at least get the boat."

Mari started, glancing at him with a raised brow. Knowing what she thought, he quickly raised a hand, palm out. "I meant my car. I definitely don't have any rug rats out there."

Nodding, a slight smile on her beautiful, sweet-tasting lips, she said, "Not one of those sailors with a different family in every port, then?"

"Definitely not."

Helping her on board, he got busy preparing for their trip.

"Need help?" she asked as he began rigging the main sail.

"Nah, it's routine. Why don't you go down to the galley and put the food in the cooler?" They'd stopped on the way over and picked up a bottle of wine, as well as some fruit and cheese.

"Good idea. Then I can be on the lookout for hatchets or sharp knives while I'm alone down there."

He gawked.

Chuckling, she said, "Haven't you ever seen *Dead Calm?*"

Vaguely remembering the thriller, about a psycho killing people on a boat, he replied, "Don't worry, no hatchets, no knives—except plastic ones, which should be okay for the food."

She let out an exaggerated sigh of relief, then went down to the galley, walking carefully on her high heels. He'd thought about suggesting she take them off when they got onboard, but had held his tongue. He was still intrigued by the idea of her sexy feet and looked forward to pulling those shoes off the way he usually looked forward to unbuttoning a woman's blouse.

"You are losing it," he told himself, wondering why he found every inch of her so alluring. Maybe it was that serendipity thing. Fate. Maybe it was just hormones. Could be just because she was beautiful and ballsy and smart.

Or it could have been that kiss.

Oh, that kiss. He *still* tasted her on his tongue, an hour later, and could only imagine how the rest of her would taste. He imagined it so much he almost forgot to open the seacock.

"Ready?" she asked as she came up on deck, joining him at the stern a short time later.

He nodded, gesturing to one of the built-in seats. "Better sit down until you get your sea legs. It's pretty breezy—we might hit some chop."

She did as he suggested, perching on the edge of the chair, almost bouncing in excitement as they left the marina and headed south. As he'd expected, the waves were high, but she didn't seem to mind. As if she'd done this a thousand times, she kept her body loose, letting herself roll with the sway of the craft, moving with it instead of against it. Like a born sailor.

Having explored the area many times, Danny headed for an inlet that would offer them some calmer water. They could anchor and watch the sunset there without too much worry about drift. He wanted to be able to share the moment with her, to keep his hands and his mind free to enjoy their time together.

Thinking about that, he suddenly realized something. She was the first woman, other than his sister, who'd ever set foot on his boat. His mom hated the water—at least, she had since Danny had told her he was enlisting in the navy. The other women he'd dated just hadn't ended up here for one reason or another.

"I love this," Mari said, starting to rise from her seat.

"Hold on," he told her. Unable to resist, he bent down and reached for the back of one of her shoes. "You really shouldn't be up on these."

Without a word, she leaned back in the chair, lifting

one long leg toward him. He slid the shoe off, slowly, noting the high arch, the delicate bones, the pretty pink-tipped toes.

"Okay," he admitted, "they're pretty spectacular feet."

"See? I told you."

He gently lowered her leg, lightly stroking her heel and ankle. Mari shivered, though whether that was from the breeze or the touch, he didn't know. Then she lifted her other leg and he repeated the process, wondering how she'd react if he pressed his mouth to that high arch and then kissed his way upward. Of course, her pants would get in the way. It would help if she were still wearing that skirt...and what she'd had on under that skirt earlier. Oh, yeah, that would definitely help.

Forcing himself to let go, he returned his focus to sailing. It wasn't the kind of clear, smooth day where he could allow himself a brief distraction. Fortunately, they were close to the inlet, and as he eased *Jazzie Girl* into it, he noted theirs was the only craft in sight. That was one thing he liked about this site—nobody else seemed to have stumbled across it.

"Pretty," Mari said as she stood beside him, holding the rail and peering at the tree-studded shoreline nearby. Then she looked toward the western sky. "Oh, wow. What a sunset!"

"Give me a minute and we'll go out on the bow. It should be calm enough to sit out there."

She pointed toward the front of *Jazzie Girl*. "The bow—that's the front, right?"

"Right."

It took a few minutes, but once he'd lowered the anchor and confirmed the steadiness of the deck, he finally nodded and gave his full, undivided attention to his passenger. She hadn't gone out to the bow. Instead she'd gone down into the galley and reappeared on deck a few minutes later with the bottle of wine—now open—and two glasses. "Thirsty?"

"Half a glass," he told her. "I don't drink and sail."

She nodded, pouring two small glasses of ruby-red wine, then handing one to him. Danny took it, sipped once, watching her do the same. Mari sighed deeply, her lips drenched red, then turned again toward the sun sinking low in the western sky. The breeze kicked up, whipping her clothes audibly against her body, and she shivered.

Danny stepped closer, for warmth. "You okay?"

"Better than," she told him, sounding fully in tune with the moment—the sensations of warmth and chill brushing her skin, the roll of the deck beneath her feet, the faint rasp of the leaves rustling on the nearest trees.

Mari, he suddenly realized, was a woman who truly savored every sight, sound, taste and touch. He had absolutely no doubt she'd be an incredibly sensual lover, and he swallowed, hard, wanting her so badly he could taste it.

The wind picked up a strand of her soft hair and blew it across his cheek. Danny inhaled the sweet, flowery smell of her shampoo blended with the warm, sultry scent of woman and had to grip the railing even tighter.

She didn't seem to notice, moving even closer beside him and covering his hand with hers, squeezing as the sun dropped a bit farther. "There it goes."

"Mmm-hmm," he acknoweldged through a nearly closed throat.

"It's as if the last drops of sunlight are falling like a slow rain shower," she mused, her deep, even breaths telling him how much she was enjoying the salty air. "I'd like to stand here naked and let it drench me."

Shit. It was a wonder the railing didn't snap...or that his fingers didn't.

Between one breath and the next, the enormous orb disappeared, pulling with it the long streams of gold that had been strewn across the water. They were left staring at a sky streaked with purple and gold, an endless watercolor painting.

He glanced at Mari, and she turned at the same moment, her smile joyful, her eyes gleaming. "That was the most beautiful sunset I have ever seen," she said, sounding delighted.

"Yeah," he muttered. "Gorgeous."

She must have seen something in his own stare, or heard it in his voice. It was something he'd been trying to hide, to control, because her own smile faded and her eyes narrowed the tiniest bit. She dropped her gaze to his mouth, then licked her lips in an unintended invitation.

That was all he'd been waiting for. Danny slid his hands into her hair and cupped her head, pulling her toward him so he could claim her mouth. She didn't hesitate, melting into his body, wrapping her arms around his neck. Their mouths came together, hot, deep and crazy... nothing like the kiss in the restaurant earlier. It was as if everything they'd both been thinking, feeling, since the minute they'd met all those hours ago had finally fallen away and they were right back to the start, dealing with that electric, instant attraction.

"God, I want you," he muttered, then he went back to tasting every corner of her mouth.

She writhed against him, her hips glued to his, her warm, full breasts tantalizing him through their clothes.

Their tongues mated in a frenzy; he wanted to taste every bit of her. Memorize the cheeks and the teeth and never—ever—forget the way she tasted. Like wine and woman and sunshine and the sea.

They didn't say it, didn't speak it. She merely reached for his shirt and tugged it free from his pants, then slipped her cool hands against his bare stomach. He hissed against her mouth, not because they were cold, but because her touch burned him right to his core.

"Do you want to go inside?" he asked, not really wanting to but not wanting her to get too cold, either.

"No," she mumbled against his mouth. "It's too small. Too closed-in." She pulled away from him enough to tug at her own shirt. "I want you here. Now."

"Thank God," he muttered. Reaching into his pocket, he grabbed the condom he'd stuck there earlier—just in case.

Spying it, she smiled. "I got some while I was shopping."

"Smart minds."

"Uh-huh."

Then there were no more words to say. He brushed her shaking hands away from her shirt and pulled it free of her waistband, tugging it straight up and off her. Danny felt his pulse ratchet up at the sight of her, clad in a lacy bra that didn't do much to conceal the jutting tips of her breasts. Unable to wait, he bent down and covered one with his mouth, tasting her through the fabric, letting her feel the warmth of his breath.

Mari nearly went out of her head, loving the heat as he began to suck her nipple. It was indescribably good— her breasts were very sensitive, anyway, and the layer of lace added to the sensation. "Oh, yes," she muttered, tightening her fingers in his golden-brown hair, liking the texture of it against her skin. Actually, there wasn't anything about him she didn't like against her skin.

He moved to her other breast, and she hissed, both at how good it felt and at the coolness of the night air against her damp bra. As if he knew what made her shudder, he lifted a hand, sliding the shoulder strap down and catching her breast in his hand. He tweaked her nipple between his fingers, drawing it to an even tighter tip of utter sensation, even as he continued to suckle the other one.

Mari groaned, helpless to do anything but *love* it as he undid her bra and dropped it to the deck, revealing her full, swaying breasts to the evening air and his covetous attention. He moved his mouth back and forth between them, as if he just couldn't decide which he liked better, and every kiss, every stroke, sent her further out of her mind.

"Please," she said, filled with pleasure, but needing more.

He straightened and kissed her mouth. "Can't help it. You're delicious."

"I'm also half-naked, and you're still fully dressed."

She reached for his shirt again and helped him pull it off, over that broad chest and those impossibly wide shoulders. Though she wanted to touch, taste and explore, first she simply had to stare at him, shocked by how utterly mouthwatering he was. She'd had lovers before, but never—ever—had she seen one who made her want to drop to her knees and beg for the chance to touch him.

Of course, if she dropped to her knees, she'd do more than touch him, she could guarantee that. She'd never been a big oral sex fan, but right now, she was dying to taste every bit of him, to experience every possible expression of sexual intimacy that existed.

Stepping back, Danny reached for his belt and unfastened it, as if he didn't trust himself to let her do it. Seeing the way her own hand shook as she reached up to stroke his arm, which bulged with muscle, she figured that was probably a good thing. She was feeling utterly ravenous, practically ready to dive on the man. If she touched, she'd take, right then and there, of that she had no doubt.

She held her breath as he unzipped his pants, revealing his bulging boxer-briefs. They couldn't even contain the tip of his erection; it jutted above the fabric.

"Oh, my," she whispered, sagging back against the back of her chair as she acknowledged how big he was. Her legs felt weak. Any fleeting concerns that she might not be able to accomodate him disappeared as her already damp sex flooded with instant heat. Her muscles clenched reflexively, already anticipating taking him, inch by devastating inch.

His wicked smile gleamed in the twilight, as if he knew exactly how he affected her. "If you don't want me to rip your pretty new pants, you'd better take them off," he told her, his tone silky, hot, sexy.

"Aye-aye, captain," she replied, though her retort was much more obedient than saucy. She was ready to do anything he asked, give him whatever he wanted, if only he filled her up, soon. She hadn't even been aware she was so incredibly empty—hollow—until she saw him. Now she could think of nothing else.

She undid the pants and pushed them down, taking her panties with them, and soon stood completely bare before him. His wolfish smile faded and his hand shook as he lifted it to rub his jaw. He raked a slow, devouring stare over her, as if trying to decide where to start. Top? Bottom? Somewhere in between?

"Take me," she ordered. "Just take me. Right now."

"No way, beautiful. Got way too much to do first."

She whimpered, thrilled beyond belief with the images of what he wanted to do with her—to her—but so desperate to have that massive ridge of male heat inside her she thought she might die.

Wanting to at least feel him in her hand, to see if she could even close it around him, she stepped closer and reached for his elastic waistband. She tugged it down, letting the back of her fingers brush against the smooth, warm skin, silky soft yet covering utter steel, and drew in a satisfied breath when he quivered in reaction.

"I'd say we both have a lot to do," she whispered.

Oh, such a lot. So damn much.

She took as much as she could of him into her palm and stroked, hearing him hiss out a low, controlled breath. If she had her way, he wouldn't maintain that control for long.

"Wait…"

"You're the one who wanted to do lots of other things."

"Yeah, I wanted to do them to you."

"Fair's fair," she insisted as she slowly stroked him, letting his body's moisture dampen her palm, making each stroke more slick and easy. She liked giving him pleasure, liked the tiny groans coming from his throat and the way the cords of muscle in his neck stood out as he dropped his head back and closed his eyes, giving himself over to it.

He didn't let her pleasure him for long, though, finally pushing her hand away and holding her by the wrist. Mari smiled in triumph, knowing he was on the edge and was as desperate as she was. He quickly tore the rest of his clothes off, then moved to her, the warmth of their naked bodies blasting away any remnants of evening chill.

"You're so beautiful," she told him, meaning it.

Marissa had never realized a man could be beautiful…but this one was. Even though his body was marked by a few scars, including a large one that ran from his hip down to his upper thigh, they only added to his masculine appeal.

He laughed softly. "That's my line."

"No line." She drew her gaze back to his face as he moved in to kiss her again, deeply. Then he moved down her body, kissing every inch of her skin, rubbing his lips here and his tongue there. The here's felt good, the there's divine.

When he got to her pelvis, he pushed her onto the chair. She shivered in anticipation, wondering where he'd go next. But he didn't delve into her core, he proceeded farther down her leg. Reaching her feet, he tasted his way all the way down to her toes, nibbling them and whispering, "You evil woman, you've given me a foot fetish."

A sultry laugh escaped her mouth, but not for long. She was well past the point of amusement. The desperation had grown second by second, until now, she was a live wire, incendiary, ready to burst into flames. As he lowered her foot and began moving his way back up her quivering thighs, she said, "Danny, I *am* going to have you now."

"Is that so?" he asked, his eyes gleaming and anticipatory.

She didn't answer with words, just with action. Sliding out of the chair, she pushed him onto his back, then slid her legs over his lean hips, cradling his cock between her thighs.

"Yeah. That's so." She slid up and down, cupping him with the lips of her sex, moistening that ridge of pulsing heat. The skin-on-skin contact was delicious, and it was with real regret that she reached for the condom he'd left nearby. She dropped the thing twice while trying to open it, so desperate to have him she could barely think straight.

"Let me," he said, taking it from her fingers. "Much longer and we're not going to need it."

She cocked a brow. "If you let this end too quickly, we're just going to have to start all over again."

He reached up and twined his fingers in her hair, drawing her down for a kiss. Before their lips touched, he whispered, "It's not going to end quickly...and we are gonna start all over again once it's over."

Which sounded like a very good plan to her.

They kissed deeply, and once she was sure he was sheathed, Marissa began to slide over him, letting her body become accustomed to him, inch by inch. Danny's muscles quivered and strained, and she knew he was holding back, letting her set the pace and the depth, making sure she was okay.

Part of her wanted him to grab her hips and thrust up into her with every ounce of strength he possessed. Another part loved the slowness of it, the anticipation of that moment when they'd be fully joined, when he'd be buried to the hilt, imprinting himself deep inside her body, where no one had ever been before.

"God help me," he groaned as she continued to inch down.

That—his audible desperation, finally drove away her last bit of restraint. She couldn't resist him, had to give them both what they wanted. She thrust down, taking him all the way inside her, throwing her head back on a shocked gasp as he filled her to the utter brim.

"You okay?" he asked, cupping her cheek and looking up at her in tender passion.

She nodded. "Like I said, it's been a while."

And she'd *never* had a man as generously built as this one.

"You set the pace," he told her.

She nodded, knowing he wouldn't do anything to hurt her. So she slowly began to ride him, taking him in tiny thrusts and grinds, not pulling all the way off him and slamming down again, though that's where they were headed. She knew she'd need it hard and deep sooner or later, but for now there was just such sweet possession, she wanted to savor it until the madness consumed her.

Her first orgasm hit her hard, completely out of the blue. It had been building, of course, but it usually took much longer for her to get there. She shuddered, gasping as currents and eddies of pleasure washed through her entire body, from the top of her head to the tips of her toes.

"Oh, yes," she whispered, sagging onto him.

As if knowing she'd gone boneless, weak, Danny rolled them over, never letting their bodies separate. The wood planking of the deck was hard and cool against her skin, and the amazing man on top of her took care not to rest his weight on her. His thick arms flexing as he bore his weight, he began to slowly thrust into her, while pressing his mouth to her cheek, her neck, her lips.

"More," she told him, "please, more."

As if he'd only been waiting to be invited, he thrust hard, then harder still. Feeling almost joyful, like she was flying, she rose to meet every powerful thrust, taking all of him over and over, until a high keening cry left her mouth as she came again.

This time, she wasn't alone. Danny shuddered, burying his face in her hair, whispering her name. One final powerful stroke, and a deep, guttural groan, told her he'd let the current carry him away, too.

Collapsing onto his side, he tugged her against him, cradling her, their arms and legs tangled. Mari made no effort to pull away, knowing this wasn't the end.

It was only the beginning.

THEY SPENT THE NIGHT on the water, curled up together in the small bed below deck. The size of the bed really didn't matter much, considering they were twined around each other throughout the entire night. Danny had lost count of the number of times he'd gotten hard for her and slid into her warm, welcoming channel. He just knew that when the sun rose, and he saw her sleeping in his arms, he wanted her yet again.

She'd been just as passionate the last time as the first, the sparks just as electric, their joining just as fulfilling.

One thing he knew without a doubt—last night, he'd had the best sex of his entire life.

And he was not about to let her get away anytime soon.

"So," he asked as he steered the boat back into the slip at around 9:00 a.m. on Sunday, "when do you think you'll hear about the job?"

"Since they want to start the guest lectures within the next few weeks, I imagine it will be soon. Why? Hoping I'll have a dead battery again?"

He reached out and brushed her tangled hair back

behind her ear, noting the lazy, satisfied look on her face. "It's not gonna take car trouble to bring us together again, Mari."

She nibbled her bottom lip, as if unsure of his meaning. "You want to...*get together* again?"

Laughing, seeing her uncertainty, he tugged her into his arms and kissed her. "Hell, yes, I want to...get together again."

"I mean, we don't have to, it's not like you made any promises. I went into this with my eyes wide-open."

Cocking a brow, he asked, "You saying you don't want to?"

"Oh, God, no!" She shook her head so hard her jaw audibly cracked.

Glad to hear it, he kissed her again, hard, a little more possessively than before. She'd given him a scare. He hadn't thought this had been an unimportant, one-time-only thing for her, but it was good to hear her confirm it.

"Okay then. I have to make a quick trip down to Norfolk—I have to leave in a couple of hours, actually. But I'll be back by Wednesday at the latest. I'll call you then."

"Okay."

He reached into his pocket and pulled out his cell phone. "Do me a favor? Plug your phone number into my address book. I'm not going to take a chance on the wind stealing away a piece of paper with your number on it."

She did as he asked, then handed the phone back. Danny glanced at the screen, knowing he'd be dialing that number very soon. Hell, maybe even tonight. He was rapidly growing addicted to her and phone sex seemed like a good way to spend a night in a crappy bed at the Norfolk Naval Station.

"I really should go," she said. "I had to call my neighbor to ask her to check in on my cat last night, and I'd prefer to get home while she's at church. Otherwise, she'll definitely come snooping around and will notice if I come home looking like I've been well-and-truly done."

"Well and truly, huh?"

She grinned. "*So* well, *so* truly."

"Okay, you get going. I've got to batten her down."

"Do you want me to stay and help?"

He waved a hand. "Nah, get on the road. You've got a hike. I'll talk to you Wednesday. Thursday at the very latest. I promise."

Nodding, Mari brushed a kiss against his lips and whispered, "Thanks, Danny."

He grabbed her hips and kissed her more thoroughly. She was wobbling on her high heels when he finally let her go.

"You're welcome."

Smiling, she let him help her onto the dock, and walked to the parking lot. She'd left her car right beside his, and he watched her get in, lifting a hand as she drove away. He waited until her car had completely disappeared from view before he got back to work, stowing his gear, getting *Jazzie Girl* properly bedded down for the windy few days predicted.

It took a while—possibly because everywhere he turned, he was confronted with another hot memory about something he'd done with Mari the night before. It was almost an hour later before he, too, was finally ready to head home to prepare for his trip down to Norfolk.

He had just grabbed the keys and was climbing down

to the dock when his phone rang. Tugging it from his pocket, he saw his youngest brother's name, and was about to answer when his wet shoe slipped a little on the ladder. He didn't fall, or even stumble, but when he grabbed for the rung, the phone slipped out of his hand.

Danny lunged for the small device, almost catching it in midair. His fingers actually brushed against the thing. But he didn't quite make it.

The phone fell with a plop into the murky waters of the marina.

"Hell," he muttered, watching it sink beneath the surface. The phone wasn't terribly new, or expensive, so for the first second, he was only mildly annoyed.

Then something sunk in. Something that was a whole lot more important to him than spending a couple of hundred bucks on a new phone.

Mari. The woman he was rapidly becoming addicted to. The woman whose last name he didn't even know.

Her number—the only way he had to get in touch with her—was in that phone.

Which was right now resting in several inches of silt at the bottom of the Chesapeake Bay.

$$5$$

Monday 5/9/11, 07:00 a.m.
www.mad-mari.com/2011/05/09/whataday
Don't you just love spring?

I do. I swear, all day yesterday, I walked around with a smile on my face, sure I'd never seen such a beautiful day. The sky was more blue, the sun more bright, the air more clean…okay, well, scratch that. You guys know I live in Baltimore. The air's not really that clean. Ugh.

Then today, I woke up, and it was raining. Pouring. Cats and dogs and Noah's ark type stuff.

But you know what? It's still absolutely gorgeous! I'm still smiling!

I'm still very happy.

Okay, before I go on, I'll admit, I met someone pretty spectacular. Yes, this is still me, still Mad-Mari, the man-hating shrew (or so says John L. from Wyoming, who wrote me that nice, chatty email last week. John, if you ever break into my house to teach me a lesson, as you threatened to, be prepared to come face-to-face with my .22. I'm an army brat and my dad taught me to shoot when I was ten).

Back to the subject—I've never said I hated men. And I don't hate men. Remember, people, a sense of humor is your friend! Sarcasm does not equal hatred.

I've had some crappy relationships and known some real jerks and that might have started this whole Mad-Mari thing. But if you've been around here for a while, you know that's not what I'm all about. I have known some really great guys. In fact, I have two fantastic, wonderful younger brothers. I just haven't had much luck in the romance department.

My luck, it appears, has changed.

But (to quote Forrest Gump) that's all I've got to say about that. The rest of the story is strictly Noneya...as in none ya bizness. I'm not one of those kiss-and-tell types who'll spill my guts all over the internet.

Suffice it to say, I met a nice man. In fact, maybe a perfect man.

And this rainy day is suddenly looking a whole lot brighter.

Wednesday 5/11/11, 07:00 a.m.
www.mad-mari.com/2011/05/11/humpday
It's hump day!

Don't you just love that even mature, adult people use that term? Whenever I hear it on the radio, it always makes me giggle. Some people who know me in my real life would probably be horrified, but, yes, apparently there's a ten-year-old-boy's sense of humor lurking inside this grown-up exterior. Shh! Don't tell.

There's this great writer I read (actually, it's two writers, a husband-and-wife team.) They produce these supersexy Harlequin books that have definitely tided me over during some romantic dry spells. (Ahem. Uh, sorry, TMI!)

Anyway, they have a Facebook page, and every Wednesday, for hump day, they offer up a naughty quote, often by Mae West. Like, "Between two evils, I always pick the one I never tried before." Or "A dame that knows the ropes isn't likely to get tied up." (My addition: Unless she wants to!)

But here's my absolute favorite of Ms. West's words of wisdom. Might be a little too romantic for hump day (and, to be honest, for Mad-Mari). But I'm in that kind of mood.

"A man's kiss is his signature."

You got that right, Mae.

Thought for the day: Would hump day still be as much fun if it were called middle-of-the-week day?

Or, I guess for you traditionalists, we could still go with Wednesday.

Whatever you call it, hope it's a great one!

Mari

Friday 5/13/11, 07:00 a.m.
www.mad-mari.com/2011/05/13/Friday

It's Friday the 13th! Do you think it's unlucky? I never have. I'm not a big believer in luck. I much prefer the idea that you get what you want out of life because you worked hard and you deserve it. I guess I do have a bit of my father's no-nonsense blood in my veins after all.

But not too much. :)

Quick question for you: How soon is too soon to start wondering why he hasn't called yet? It's been a while since I've done this dating thing.

Thanks!

Mari

Oh, P.S. Thought for the day—do people still say dating? My teenage sister just says "hooking up." Which, to me, means something else entirely. (And the thought of my teenage sister doing that really shocks me. Yikes!) So, what do you think?

Discuss!

Monday 5/16/11, 07:00 a.m.
www.mad-mari.com/2011/05/16/goodnews
    I got the job! Yay!

Monday 5/16/11, 07:32 a.m.
www.mad-mari.com/2011/05/16/goodnews
Comment #6
    Thanks for the kudos on the job AllyBMe!
    SandyT, JLoNo, Sucrebby, Franni from Frisco…the whole point of me posting about the job, and not about him was because no, (to answer your much-repeated question) I haven't heard from him. Yet.

Monday 5/16/11, 08:45 a.m.
www.mad-mari.com/2011/05/16/goodnews
Comment #21

Thanks again for the congrats. But to those of you who are just determined to ask...no, I am NOT worried that he won't call. I don't know him well, but I know a lying scumbag when I meet one, and he's not one.

Monday 5/16/11, 07:20 p.m.
www.mad-mari.com/2011/05/16/goodnews
Comment #48

You guys really aren't making me feel any better here. Am I totally crazy to be telling myself there's a good reason I haven't heard from him? He did say he was going out of town for a few days. And I did tell him he didn't have to call.

Monday 5/16/11, 07:58 p.m.
www.mad-mari.com/2011/05/16/goodnews
Comment #62

No, Joanie from KY, of course I didn't mean it when I told him he didn't have to call. Duh!

And yes, Tiredmommy, he did promise he would.

Monday 5/16/11, 08:18 p.m.
www.mad-mari.com/2011/05/16/goodnews
Comment #70

Yeah, I'm pretty sure there are phones where he was going.

And no, I don't suppose he could have lost my number...unless his cell phone got run over by a truck or something!

Hey, anything's possible, right?

Monday 5/16/11, 10:32 p.m.
www.mad-mari.com/2011/05/16/goodnews
Comment #92

PLEASE stop trying to cheer me up about how all men are scum! I am NOT ready to concede that about this particular one. Something could have happened.

Or…not. Shit.

It's been a long day. Think I'll go drink a bottle of wine and eat a quart of Häagen-Dazs now.

P.S. Maybe he got sick?

Tuesday 5/17/11, 07:00 a.m.
www.mad-mari.com/2011/05/17/stillhope

I got a good night's sleep and woke up feeling better. I'm not ready to give up hope. There was a trip involved. And we all know crazy things can happen when you travel.

Okay, he was only traveling about a hundred miles so there's no way he lost a passport or a plane ticket or got some rare tropical disease. But still, cars do break down.

Well…okay, maybe not that one. (Can't say why—I'm trying to be discreet about who he is, remember?)

But his business could have taken longer than he expected. So I am not going to panic here. Not going to doubt my own judgment. I'm a pretty good judge of character and I'm not a pushover.

Say it with me: There's no reason to fear the worst!

Tuesday 5/17/11, 8:48 p.m.
www.mad-mari.com/2011/17/05/stillhope
Comment #73
Screw that shit. I'm fearing the worst.

Thursday 5/19/11, 07:00 a.m.
www.mad-mari.com/2011/19/05/blue
Not much to say today. Honestly, I'm feeling pretty down.
I liked this guy. A lot.
Too much, I fear.

Monday 5/23/11, 07:00 a.m.
www.mad-mari.com/2011/05/23/hell
He still hasn't called. And it's pretty obvious now that he isn't going to.
FML

6

DANNY WILKES HAD BEEN in the navy for several years. He'd trained rigorously, had flown dozens of missions, had landed multi-million-dollar aircraft on carriers hundreds of miles from shore, had endured tests of strength and endurance that would have made a lot of men quit. He'd had his plane shot out from under him and had spent a brutal day in an Afghan desert with a torn-up leg, a broken radio and about enough ammunition to take on one small enemy foot patrol. Thankfully, none had come along.

He'd done all that because he didn't know how to quit.

So he sure as hell hadn't quit trying to find *her*.

"Marissa Marshall," he muttered, glad he had finally learned her last name, at least.

It had been two weeks, and he was still kicking himself for being stupid enough to lose his phone. That was on a long list of stupid shit he'd done since meeting Mari, starting with not getting her last name. Followed by not writing down her number, or getting her address, giving her *his* number, making a date to meet her, getting in his car and racing up toward Baltimore to see if he could catch her on the road that morning—the one after the best night of sex of his life.

He hadn't gone after her; she'd had an hour's head start. She'd probably been arriving home, somewhere in downtown Baltimore, right around the time his cell had gone in the drink.

Yes. He'd been desperate enough that he'd dived into the water to look for it. Finding it was a long shot, and he was 99% sure it wouldn't work if he did, but he'd gone for it anyway.

No luck. The water was cold as shit, not to mention murky and slimy with grease and boat oil. And deep.

The trip to Norfolk had been critical, but as soon as he'd come back, he'd begun to search. He'd scoured the internet, trying to find anything he could—a graduation announcement?—for a Baltimore-area PhD, first name Marissa. *Nothing.*

He'd also tried calling in favors. He'd gotten a buddy who was dating somebody in personnel to ask around. *Zip.* He finally decided to trust in fate. Serendipity had been hard at work on the day they'd met. He didn't doubt he was meant to see her again. He just had to trust it would happen.

And it would, soon. Very soon. Because his last-ditch hope had played out. Mari had apparently landed the job here at the academy. A flyer had gone out to all the instructors last week, informing them of the upcoming guest lectures for at-risk students. Marissa *Marshall*, PhD, would be talking to the middies about how the military affected family life.

Armed with her last name, he'd searched again. He'd had more luck, finding her in a journal that had reprinted a section of her dissertation. But her number and address were unlisted. There was no contact email or website in the article and nobody at the journal answered his request for more information.

So he'd finally accepted the fact that he'd have to wait until she came to deliver her first lecture to talk to her again. Hopefully she'd give him the time of day and let him explain, instead of ignoring him, or slapping his face.

He'd find out soon. In an hour, she'd be in a lecture hall not far from where he taught his aeronautics class, his assignment during this shore rotation. Of course, the way his luck was running, it just figured that he'd been ordered to attend a hoity-toity reception for some visiting dignitaries right before she was supposed to arrive.

"So, Midas, any luck finding your mystery woman?" a voice asked.

Recognizing it as Quag—aka Quagmire—he turned to his aviator buddy and lifted a corner of his mouth. "As a matter of fact, yes. She's going to be here this morning."

The other man gestured toward Danny's dress whites. "Dressing to impress, huh? You really think that'll get her to forgive you for not calling?"

"Nope. Pure groveling is going to be required. As for the uniform—some special guests are arriving on base and I've been invited to the dog and pony show."

Whether as the dog or the pony, he wasn't quite sure. But he had no doubt he'd be paraded.

"Showing off a hotshot flyboy, huh? Why wasn't I invited?"

Danny playfully punched the other man in the shoulder. "Your call sign is Quagmire for a reason, pal. You always seem to land in them."

"Sure. Gotta have the golden boy, the one with the

Midas touch to get those guests to loosen up the purse strings, huh?"

"You forgetting I got my call sign because I'm a damn good mechanic who gets stuck fixing everybody's cars?"

"Yeah, but you know the bigwigs won't tell anybody that," Quag said with a smirk. "They want the gold, not the grease."

"I guess."

"Consider it prep work for NASA," Quag said, being one of the few who knew of Danny's hopes to get into the astronaut program. "You gotta get used to schmoozing."

True. Danny knew he had to play the game. If the brass wanted to show him off now and again, liking that medal on his chest, he'd go along.

He glanced down at the medal, feeling rather emotionless about the visible reminder of his adventure in the Afghan desert. The scar on his leg was a much more effective one.

Mari hadn't seemed at all revolted by that scar, which was, in his opinion, pretty damned ugly. During the long, sultry night hours they'd spent together, she'd touched him there, kissed the puckered flesh, murmured something sweet about how much she hated that he'd been hurt.

He swallowed hard, remembering what else she'd done when exploring that part of his body. He really needed to not think those things right now. Hopefully he'd be able to later.

Fortunately, at the time she'd discovered the scar, they'd both been...distracted. She'd asked no questions about it.

That was a good thing. Talking about that ordeal in

the desert wasn't something he enjoyed. Considering she was a shrink, it would probably be especially hard to share it with Mari. She'd be the double whammy—her female instincts trying to coddle him, like his mom and sister had. Her psychologist ones wanting to heal him.

Screw that. He was fully healed. His head was on straight and he was back where he belonged, flying Mach speed toward his future.

"Good luck, man, hope she buys your story."

"She will 'cause God knows it's the truth."

The other man grinned. "If she doesn't, send her my way. I'll tell her how crazy you've been, trying to track her down."

"You're the *last* person I'd send a woman I wanted to!"

That was only part-joke. Quag had a rep as a ladies' man.

"Oh, yeah, look who's talking. You might have turned into Mr. Straight And Narrow, but don't think I haven't heard the stories about your early years. You put me to shame, pal."

Maybe once. But not anymore. When he had been younger, more carefree, sure, he'd played the field. Like every other Naval Aviator, he had gotten a lot of female attention. Movies like *Top Gun* and *An Officer and a Gentleman* had created something of a cult status around guys like him. Which he'd always thought was really stupid…but hadn't exactly disliked when it got him the attention of girl after pretty girl.

But he was no longer a kid. No longer in his twenties. Quag wasn't, either. So maybe it wasn't just age.

Maybe it had something to do with flying out of the sky without a plane. Thinking long and hard about life and death.

Yeah. He suspected that's when he realized there was a whole lot more to life than meeting women. And ever since that time, he hadn't come across a single one who truly interested him.

Until Mari.

"Later, dude," said Quag. "Go be *charming.*"

Saying goodbye, he headed to his meeting, playing his role—the *charming* Naval Aviator. He answered the same questions every visitor asked, evaded the same flirtation from the bored-looking wives and the same hearty, I'm-a-pasty-middle-aged-guy-but-I'm-still-as-strong-as-you-are handshakes from the rich men.

He knew this was part of the job, knew it would be worse if he ever became an astronaut, so he went along. It was worth it, the way things got done. Who you knew was almost as important as what you stood for or what you could do, at least if you wanted to go any further than he'd already gone. And he did. All the way to Houston. Then, when the politicians got their heads out of their asses and realized the U.S.A. had to regain its scientific edge in space, he hoped to go straight to the moon.

Finally, after what seemed like forever but was probably not much more than an hour, he ducked out of the reception. Glancing at his watch and realizing there were only ten minutes left in Mari's lecture, he hurried across the nearly deserted grounds. This was like a different place without all the regular students. There were still a few hundred around, but, right now, most of them were attending remedial classes.

When he got to the lecture hall, he saw the door open from within, and stepped out of the way. Exiting the room was Kyle Riddick, one of the deans. Riddick was a prickly, fussy old guy, who probably had come just to make sure the new guest teacher didn't mistakenly treat

the students like young adults, rather than fifth grad-
ers, as Riddick seemed to think they should be treated.
Danny'd had run-ins with the man on more than one
occasion.

"Commander Wilkes," the other man said with a
slight nod.

"Is the lecture still going on?" Danny asked, worried
for a moment that he'd missed her.

Riddick frowned, his lips pursing tightly. "It is. And
I can't say that's a good thing. No, indeed, I cannot."

Had the remark come from anyone else, Danny might
have worried about Mari's presentation. From this guy?
He knew damn well what the problem was. Mari was
young, attractive and the students were bound to like
her. Three strikes in Riddick's eyes.

"She's far too young for this job."

Strike one.

"She's also much too attractive—those boys might
pretend they're listening, but it's obvious they're just
ogling her."

Strike two.

"And they're altogether too fresh and friendly with
her already."

And you're out.

Damn, he was good.

"She's highly qualified," Danny said, knowing it was
true.

"Perhaps," Riddick said, tsking a little. "Still, I'm
afraid I might have to do something about this. I don't
like that inexperienced young woman in a room full of
my boys without an adult present."

Danny nearly snorted. An adult? As if Mari was a
seventeen-year-old girl playing at being a teacher? Of
course, to this old geezer, she probably did seem very

young. "I think the Deputy to the Commandant is pretty impressed with her."

Pursing those lips even tighter, and crossing his arms across his narrow chest, the old man sniffed. "Well, we'll just see about that," he said, then strode away.

Fortunately, the guy was a blowhard, who kept his job by virtue of being an institution, so Danny didn't really worry about Mari's job security. Hell, if Riddick had the power to get rid of anybody he wanted to, this place would have about a third the faculty and a quarter of the students.

Hearing the murmur of voices in the lecture hall, Danny pushed the door open, and immediately realized why the campus seemed so empty. It appeared every midshipman left on campus was in this room, crowded shoulder to shoulder, filling every seat and lining the walls.

Considering every single student in the room was male, he had a feeling he knew why. And looking toward the front of the hall, seeing Mari standing at the lectern, he knew he was right.

"Damn, the bun's back," he muttered.

But, as he'd suspected, her severe hairstyle didn't matter one little bit. Mari's clothes might not be quite as tight as they'd been the day they'd met, but there was simply no disguising the fact that she was a beautiful, sexy female. It didn't matter whether the blouse outlined those breasts, or merely skimmed over them, they were still jaw-droppingly perfect. Nor did it make any difference whether her skirt clung to her hips and ass like shrink wrap or merely covered them modestly, they were still begging to be held, caressed.

Danny swallowed hard, took a few deep, steadying breaths, then slipped all the way into the room, remaining near the door. He didn't want to distract her, and he sensed he would be a distraction. Probably an unwelcome one, considering she had to think he was an asshole for not calling. Hopefully, though, she'd hear him out and let him take her to lunch to apologize.

"Now," he heard her say, "are there any questions?"

Hands immediately shot up. Not surprisingly, the first few midshipmen made suggestive or flirtatious comments. Dr. Marshall shot them down carefully, not being cruel but brooking no nonsense, either. But it wasn't until one came out and asked her if she was single that she sighed in visible annoyance.

Staring at the back of the student's head, Danny cleared his throat. The young man glanced around, saw him in the crowd, and all the color fell out of his ruddy cheeks.

Mari didn't seem to notice. "Not that it's your business," she said, her hard gaze traveling over the room, "but yes, I'm single. And no, I'm not interested, even if you weren't way too young for me, which all of you are."

The young man lowered his head, not replying, either because he'd been shot down or because he knew Danny, one of his regular teachers, was staring at him from ten feet away.

"Maybe you haven't been listening to what I've said for the past hour," Mari added, "so let me repeat myself. Maintaining a relationship with someone in the military is *hard*. A lot of people simply aren't interested."

A voice called, "I bet one of us could change your mind!"

"Oh, right, because you're such Prince Charmings," she said with an exaggerated shrug that managed to look more amused than annoyed. "Believe me, I have two younger brothers, I'm wise to you all. I've noticed every note, every text, every piece of paper thrown and every smirk today."

The young men laughed good-naturedly, obviously already liking her. She had developed a rapport with them. Their comments were flirtatious, but there was an underlying respect. Nobody was crossing the line. And as long as they didn't cross it, she seemed willing to talk to them on their terms, on their level.

"Now, back to the question. You think some girl— leaving me totally out of this conversation—is going to just rush out to get involved with a sailor?"

"Hell, yeah!" someone called.

She walked to the edge of the floor, looking from face to face. "Sorry to break it to you, but not a lot of women will line up to be with an adrenaline junkie who risks his life every single day for a government worker's salary."

The young men in the room stilled.

"One who sees some pretty awful stuff and might have a hard time leaving his job at the office when it's time to come home to her at night."

A few glances were exchanged.

"One who will be gone for months or years at a time. Who will drag her and their kids all over the world, leaving her lonely, cut off and eventually resentful. Why do you think divorce rates in the military skyrocketed in the last decade?"

The students were listening carefully, he could see that in the expressions of those closest to him.

"It's a rough life and a lot of women just don't want it. They see a man in uniform and turn and walk the other way."

Wow. Danny couldn't help hearing the simple honesty

in her voice. Remembering what she'd said about her own family, he knew she meant every word she'd said.

But she couldn't be *too* serious about it. After all, she'd gone home with him, spent the night in his arms. So perhaps she was just emphasizing the downsides to the students to make sure they got the message.

"So what are we supposed to do?" asked one young man, a quiet one who was in Danny's class. A good kid, deep thinker, but one who just hadn't mastered the discipline. It made sense that he'd be one of the first to realize this sexy lecturer had some really valuable information to impart.

"That's what I'm here to talk to you about, and the point I've been trying to make to you. I want to help you see those problems coming at you and take steps to avoid them."

"Meaning, get used to being single!" a voice called.

She laughed gently and shook her head. "Not necessarily. You need to learn to talk openly with someone you care about, to make sure you're both on the same page about what you want and your long-term plans. How to keep the lines of communication open during long separations."

"Yeah, making sure she doesn't cheat while you're gone!" someone said.

She shrugged, not denying the possibility. "Or making sure *you* don't cheat when you're lonely and far from home."

Wow, that one had to have hit home with her. She hadn't talked much about her parents situation, beyond admitting infidelity had been the catalyst that had driven her mother out. But he knew the subject had to be a sensitive one.

But everything she said was dead-on, Danny knew

that from watching his buddies over the years. They worried about their girls back home. Then they got lonely and accepted a welcoming embrace from one of the nameless women who always hovered around military hangouts.

If these lectures really could help some of these kids go into this knowing what they'd be dealing with, he considered that a very good thing.

"There's also the matter of respecting women," she added. "Since you're all male, I'd like to talk about that, too. We all know there have been some scandals in the past regarding sexual discrimination."

Oh, boy, had there. These young men had had that message hammered home since day one. The navy had never forgotten the Tailhook scandal, which had brought down dozens of officers accused of sexual harassment of their female colleagues.

Mari's voice lowered as she added, "You're taught to be officers and gentlemen, and you really need to respect that code. Be as respectful to women in the outside world as you are to those in the military. Be honest and direct, leave the bad-boy-player games for the civilians. Rise above the urge to take what you want and never call, and maybe those character lessons will help you deal with your relationships later in your careers."

Ouch. Direct hit. Danny shifted a little, wanting to see her face, and the tight frown he saw told him he was right. She was speaking from personal experience.

And judging by the tension of her pose, and the deepening frown, she was pissed.

He took a sideways step, approaching the door, figuring he'd better get out of here before she saw him. A private conversation was definitely in order.

But fate and a jumpy sophomore trying to get a better

look conspired against him. The kid lurched right just as Danny stepped left. Something—maybe his dress whites—drew the attention of the instructor, and kept it.

Their stares met and locked. He noted the paleness of her cheeks, the faint, dark smudges under her eyes that probably went unnoticed by everyone else in the room, but spoke to him of sleepless nights. God, he hoped he wasn't responsible for them.

Nothing could take away from the prettiness of her face, though. It felt so good to look directly at her after their separation and his fear that he'd never see her again, he couldn't prevent a smile from widening his lips.

She didn't return it. "What the...?" she mumbled.

Her eyes flared, then slowly narrowed as she gazed at him in silence. Then she raked a thorough stare over him, head to toe. Even from here, he noticed the way her hands shook as she saw him in full uniform for the first time.

As if the sight truly shocked her, Mari's mouth dropped open so hard it might have hurt. Obviously she meant it when she'd said she didn't like men in uniform. It was a damn shame he had to visibly remind her that she didn't like soldiers or sailors before he'd gotten her to forgive him for not contacting her. He wished he'd changed before coming to find her. But he couldn't have wasted even the few minutes that would have taken.

Unable to take the staring contest anymore, Danny lifted a hand in a small wave, his expression hopefully saying what he couldn't say out loud. That he was very glad to see her, and had sought her out so they could talk.

She didn't wave in return. Or smile. She merely continued to stare. Her mouth was open, her shoulders rising as she sucked in deep breaths. As if she'd become light-headed, she reached back to put a steadying palm on the lectern.

"You okay, Doc?" a voice asked.

A brief hesitation, then she stiffened, remembering her audience. "I'm fine, thanks." Jerking herself into a ramrod straight posture, she dropped her hand to her side and her gaze went back to her students.

He had no doubt, however—none at all—that every bit of her mental focus was entirely on him.

And those weren't happy thoughts she was thinking.

MARISSA DIDN'T KNOW WHICH infuriated her more: That Danny had shown up here, or that he was…was…damn it, what was he?

A navy officer.

Yeah. He had to be. Halloween was a long way off, and no way would he be walking around the USNA wearing that uniform unless he was entitled to it. Which meant her heroic Midas man wasn't a mechanic at all. He wasn't a simple, supersexy, blue collar guy, the kind on her "safe" list.

Not that he was safe, under any circumstances. Not for her mental health. Not for her physical health, either. She'd been walking around for two weeks with a head-ache and a huge knot in her stomach.

And he definitely wasn't good for her heart. Because, whether he'd known all along that he had no intention of calling her, or he'd just changed his mind after she left that morning, the organ in the center of her chest had taken a major hit. It still ached. Throbbed, actually, now that she was seeing him in the flesh.

No. Not in the flesh. In the uniform.

Damn him. For not calling, for hurting her, for giving her an amazing night that she'd never forget, knowing it would never be repeated.

Damn him for looking so incredibly good in those pristine clothes. The tailor-made uniform emphasized those broad shoulders and lean hips, the whole ensemble making him look like the ultimate hero.

Damn him most of all for lying about who he was. She didn't care how attractive she'd found him that first day. If she'd had any idea he was a military man, she would never have asked him to lunch. And she definitely would never have gone back to his boat with him. His uniform made him look like an officer and a gentleman—in reality, he was a womanizer and a liar. She should know. She'd been his woman…and she'd been lied to.

"So, Doc, what do you do when you meet the hottest girl you've ever seen, but she has a thing against sailors?" a young voice asked.

Marissa couldn't prevent an instinctive reply. "You don't deceive her, that's for sure."

"What do you mean?" the student asked.

She tore her thoughts away from Danny and addressed the earnest-looking young man in the second row. "Don't ever hide who you really are. I can't tell you what will work, but I can tell you what *won't*."

"What's that?"

"Pretending to be something else, to try to manipulate her into liking you before you admit you're in the service. She'll be doubly angry when she finds out—and the two strikes that uniform might have cost you when you went up to bat become three with that lie. It will put you out of the game altogether."

She couldn't prevent a quick, sideways glance at

Danny, wondering if he felt the heat of her stare through her half-lowered lids.

He flinched.

Yeah. He felt it.

"But how do you get her to even get to know you if she shoots you down as soon as she finds out what you do?"

"Maybe you don't," Marissa said, being blunt, both because she was still angry at Danny, and because these kids really needed to know the truth. "Maybe you just move on to somebody else. Because getting involved with someone under false pretenses is a surefire way to doom any relationship."

A deep throat clearing brought her attention back to the tall, incredibly handsome man in white, who was walking through the crowd toward the front of the room. The students melted around him, clearing a path. She saw several grins, and heads coming together in whispers, indicating Danny was well-liked.

Well, goody for him.

"It's the Midas man," somebody muttered.

Midas man? She stiffened, more confused than before.

"Mind if I jump in?" he asked, his voice smooth and calm. She, apparently, was the only one feeling like a complete wreck at this unexpected interaction.

Of course, it hadn't been unexpected for him. There had been no surprise in his expression when their stares had met. She suspected he'd come here, knowing he'd find her, though why, she couldn't say. He'd been brushing her off for weeks. Why bother to seek her out now?

Maybe he's horny.

Yeah. Maybe. If so, she just hoped he was on a first-name basis with his own hand, because he sure wasn't getting any satisfaction from her.

Neither are you.

Right. No satisfaction for her, either. That hurt a little to think about because, to be honest, she didn't think she'd ever been with a man who'd satisfied her more.

But it wasn't happening. Not ever again. *Fool me once, shame on you. Fool me twice and I give up Mad-Mari.com and change my website to Stupid-Mari.*

Danny didn't wait for permission before speaking. "You all know lying is never the right way to go." He glanced around at the others in the crowded room, then back at the first boy, who sat just a few feet away from Mari. And when he spoke, she knew he was talking as much to her as to the students. "But having a mature, trusting relationship goes both ways. You each have to not only be honest, but you have to be willing to *listen.*"

Listen. Huh. That honey-tongued man was far too easy to listen to, that was part of the problem!

"If you make a mistake, and want to set things right, you have to hope the person with whom you want to make amends is willing to hear you out," he added.

"That only works if you actually have a decent, reasonable excuse," Marissa added.

He finally gave her his full attention, those amber eyes glistening with the intensity of his stare. "And how are you going to know whether the excuse is decent and reasonable unless you give him a chance to explain?"

She turned to face him, as well. "Some things don't require explanation."

"Like?"

"Like lying about who you are and what you do. That is inexcusable."

"Whose to say somebody lied? I mean, did the actual words leave his mouth? Did he tell this girl, 'I'm not in the navy,' or did she just assume it?"

She hesitated.

As if not realizing the two adults in the room were shooting comments back and forth to each other, the boy said, "You mean, like, if I just met somebody at a club and wasn't with my boys or in uniform and it just didn't come up?"

Danny nodded. "Something like that."

"No, it's nothing like that," she insisted.

"How do you know?" Danny asked. "How can you be sure if you won't let him explain things?"

Hesitating, Marissa quickly thought back to the day they'd met. To their conversation, their every interaction. Had he ever actually *said* he was a mechanic, or that he was just visiting the base? Or that the name on his mechanic's overalls didn't mean what she thought it meant?

The Midas Man.

Gold hair. Sexy, confident, strong, smart. Immaculately uniformed…with, oh, God, was that a set of wings on his collar?

The truth washed over her.

Son of a bitch. Her good-with-his-hands mechanic was a navy pilot. An elite, reckless, danger-loving, highly romanticized flyboy who probably had women throwing themselves at him every single day—at least, they certainly did in the movies. She'd probably been just another walk in the park—or a roll on the deck—to him.

Those greasy coveralls? Apparently a flight suit.

The word she'd taken for a company logo?

"Midas is your call sign," she whispered.

He heard. And nodded once.

She closed her eyes for a second, trying to pull her thoughts together. Yes, she'd obviously made a big assumption...but he could have corrected it. Correction: he *should* have corrected it. She very easily recalled their conversation about the military, when she'd mentioned her family, told him she'd broken a rule by dating a soldier. Could he really have been using pure semantics to think she didn't mean a sailor, as well?

Tilting her chin up, she opened her eyes and struggled to remain cool and impassive.

Sticking his hand out, obviously for the benefit of their audience, he said, "Lieutenant Commander Danny Wilkes. Aka Midas."

Unable to do anything else, Marissa lifted hers, as well. The brush of skin on skin was electric, like it had been from the very start, and she pulled away as quickly as she could, certain her fingertips had been singed by the heat of him. She didn't like that he affected her still, when she'd spent the past several days trying hard to get over him. She'd almost convinced herself that she'd had a night of great sex and shouldn't have expected anything more, anyway. *Almost.*

Trouble was, she had expected more. He'd made her expect more.

Even worse, she'd wanted more. He'd made her want more.

Shaking off the images flooding her head, she got right back to the point—to the realization she'd quickly made, even after acknowledging she'd been the one who'd jumped the gun that day they'd met. "Okay, so maybe she makes a foolish assumption. But maybe he shouldn't keep his big mouth shut and play innocent when the conversation turns to how much she dislikes men in the military."

"Present company excepted?" Danny asked.

She caught her lip between her teeth and looked at the faces of the suddenly-more-interested young men. "Of course, I was talking in generalities, not about anyone here."

"So was I," he retorted. "I mean, what if he figured she was making a general statement, not talking specifically about him. Because as far as he can tell, why *wouldn't* she know who he is and what he does?"

She shook her head, a little confused, not to mention still very jumpy.

Another boy piped in. "But she doesn't, 'cause they just met at a club and he's not with his boys or in uniform."

Danny turned to the student. "But say she met him on base and he was on KP and wearing a kitchen smock… and she assumes he's a cook."

"You've got to be kidding me." Marissa closed her eyes briefly, knowing exactly where he was going.

He spelled it out. "So how's he supposed to know she'd make that assumption if she didn't say, 'Hey, how do you like being a cook?' He's in his everyday element. Would it immediately occur to him that she'd assume he was something else?"

"Maybe not," she whispered, realizing it was true.

Danny had to have been in the navy for a very long time if he was a pilot. Which meant his job had become part of his persona. He was on a navy base, wearing what she now knew had been some kind of uniform. So of course his natural assumption would have been that it was pretty obvious he belonged there.

"No," he said, his voice almost as low as hers. "Maybe not. So is he still a really bad guy for not realizing what she thought and spelling it out?"

Marissa's attitude softened the tiniest bit—there was no denying the warmth in his expression. She believed him, on this at least. She'd been the one who'd made a pretty big assumption, one which he hadn't even recognized.

"I suppose he isn't," she admitted.

Danny smiled, then turned to the boys. "See? Talking, listening, they're good skills to have."

Especially if you talked as sweetly as the smooth-tongued man beside her.

She stiffened, her defenses remaining high. Because he was good at this—sweet-talking. He was so charming, so quick-witted. Sure, his reasoning had been good, but would she have fallen for it as readily if this conversation had been with anyone less adept at using words to his advantage?

Maybe. Or maybe not.

And maybe if it had *just* been the job thing, she could let this go, as he seemed to want her to. No, things could never go much further between them than sex—his job *was* an issue, whether he'd lied about it or not. But the sex had been pretty damned spectacular and there were worse ways to *have fun* with someone, even if there was no future in it.

The fact remained, however, that he hadn't called. No biggie if he hadn't promised he would. Well, it would have been a biggie to her, because whatever she'd said about it at the time, she had truly wanted him to.

The point was, he *had* promised. He'd made her believe he was desperate to see her again. Not just saying he'd call, but asking her to plug in her number so he wouldn't possibly lose it, giving her a specific day on which she'd hear from him.

He hadn't followed through. And it had hurt. Badly.

The cyber-blood she'd spilled on her website during that time was a stark reminder of just how much she had been hurt.

The very fact that it had hurt her so much meant it was time to cut her losses. Sex for fun's sake was one thing. Sex with someone who had the power to hurt her—one she knew she had no future with—was another thing entirely.

Maybe the twenty-two-year-old Mad-Mari would have taken the risk and just gone for a great sexual affair. But the adult Marissa, who was moving on to the next phase of her life, just wasn't willing to do it.

"That's a very good point," she finally said, eyeing Danny, then casting her attention toward the class. "The scenario Dan...er, Commander Wilkes shared is a good example of how miscommunication can affect relationships."

That sexy mouth widened a tiny bit, and his tense posture might have eased, too. As if he really cared about her response.

Which she might have believed...if he hadn't blown her off after she'd left that morning.

"So you...she, wouldn't hold it against him?" he asked, obviously wanting it written in stone.

"Maybe not that," she conceded.

He pressed his advantage. "And at least if she's not upset about that, she might stick around long enough to get to know you, give you a chance to tell her some things she might need to hear."

She shrugged. Keeping her tone cool, she replied, "Maybe. Or maybe she's just not interested in hearing any more. But at least you haven't lied about it. The important thing is, don't make promises you don't intend to keep." She shot him a direct stare. "And once she makes it clear that she's not interested, you need to let it go and move on."

His mouth tightened, and she'd swear she heard a sigh of frustration, even as the students took up the conversation amongst themselves.

Then she definitely heard something else.

Him. Muttering two words.

"Like hell."

7

Monday, 5/23/10, 07:05 p.m.
www.mad-mari.com/2011/05/23/onedown

Well, I made it through day one on the job, and I think it went pretty well. Most importantly, I liked it. Not getting into specifics here, but I have to say I think I've found something I might be really good at. Or, at least, a group I am good at working with.

Sounds cryptic, I know. Sorry. I really have to keep my real life separate from my cyber one.

Here's something interesting…I ran into Mr. Perfect.

No, he didn't explain why he didn't call. Well, actually, I didn't give him a chance to. He tried to talk to me as I was leaving, but ended up getting called over by some bigwig, so I made my getaway. Yes, that's me, the chickenshit. Figured it was better to play it cool and act like I don't care enough to want an explanation than to be a blubbery girl and be all self-righteous about it.

Interestingly, though, we did have a chance to speak, albeit in front of an audience. And it turns out I made a pretty big mistake the day we met. So while I can still think he's a numero uno creeper for blowing me off the morning after, I can't be mad at him for...something else.

Argh! I know it's frustrating that I can't expound—it frustrates me, too. But trust me, I can't. Heaven forbid this guy ever find out who I am and stumble over this blog. Can you imagine him reading my entries over the past couple of weeks, when I've done something I NEVER do—pretty much spilled my heart all over the web? :shudder:

Interestingly, I kinda think he cared about me forgiving him. It mattered to him.

And I suspect he might even have wanted to see me again. But considering how blue I felt after he didn't call, no way am I gonna travel down Excitement Road into Ditched-and-Heartbroken Valley again.

Anyway, I'm feeling better on one hand, worse on the other. Why does trying to be smart and sensible leave you feeling so damned miserable? Discuss!

Have a good one—
Mari

DANNY ARRIVED ON MARISSA'S street at 6:30 the next evening, wondering what kind of reaction he was going to get when he knocked on her apartment door.

A good, solid slam probably had the highest odds.

A welcoming kiss? About slim to none.

But that didn't deter him. He had to see her, to explain things to her. That last zinger in the classroom today told him she had her back up and wasn't going to make it easy on him. But hell, the best things in life never came easily.

Besides, he had another reason to talk to her—and it had nothing to do with them, personally.

"Damn you, Riddick," he mumbled, not for the first time. It appeared the old dean had managed to actually cause some trouble this time—trouble aimed directly at Marissa.

Though, to be honest, he had to give credit where it was due—Riddick might be an ass, but he'd done Danny a favor today. Because the man's complaints had actually enabled Danny to get Mari's address. When the Deputy to the Commandant had asked Danny to his office late this afternoon, and shared Riddick's concerns—and the deputy's solution—Danny had been ready to kiss them both. Not only because Danny now had the perfect excuse to ask for Mari's contact information, but because he also had a solid reason to spend time with her.

Hopefully, there would be enough time for him to explain about his phone…and get her to agree to give him another chance. Knowing now that she had a serious thing against any man in uniform had pushed the obstacle even higher, but he wasn't about to give up without at least making sure she knew he hadn't blown her off.

Arriving at her place in downtown Baltimore, he hoped she didn't live in a high-security building, where he'd have to buzz her to get her to let him in. He suspected she wouldn't do it and he'd be left trying to sneak in behind another resident. That was all he needed, getting arrested as a stalker. Wouldn't that look great to NASA.

Right now, though, he couldn't think about that. He could only think about the look on Mari's face when she'd made those comments about *not keeping promises* and *not being interested*. He had to talk to her. Just *had* to.

Fortunately, the building was an older one, though it looked well kept and was on a nice, safe-looking street. But there was no real security at the entrance. He got in without any difficulty, made his way up to her door, and knocked.

A few seconds passed. Then a full minute. Silence filled the hall, not a sound came from behind the closed door.

He knocked again. "Mari? It's Danny, I need to talk to you. Please let me in." Wondering if it might help, he added, "It's about work."

Nada. He didn't think he'd have heard a mouse stirring.

"Don't give up, hon, she's in there," said a voice thick with that oh-so-distinctive Baltimore accent. Or, in local terminology, Bal'mer.

Turning, Danny saw an older woman watching him from her own doorway next door. He had to wonder if this was the one Mari had called to take care of her cat—the nosy one who would have noticed what time Mari got home that Sunday morning.

"Excuse me?"

"Marissa, I mean. She's home, I heard her shower running through the walls not twenty minutes ago."

"Thin walls," he muttered.

"That's what Marissa says, every time she complains about me listening to my afternoon stories!" the woman exclaimed, sounding indignant. "I don't know why she doesn't like them, that Erica on *All My Children* is a hootenanny and a half. And there's lots of good romance and stuff on there." The woman wagged her eyebrows. "She could use some of that."

He managed to hide a grin. "Thanks."

"So, anyway, she's in there," the woman insisted. "I would have heard her door if she'd left."

"Oh, okay…"

"So you should knock again."

Nosy neighbor much? He suddenly felt for Mari, who was, he suspected standing on the other side of the door, eyeing him through the peephole. She'd probably been trying to avoid him and was now torn between wanting to stay there so he'd go away, or open the door and yank him in just to get him away from her gabby old neighbor.

He could be nice and just leave. But damned if he was going without giving it one more shot.

And there's still the other little matter to discuss.

Which might not make her happy, either. Especially if she didn't get over her anger at him.

As if suddenly struck by something—maybe some common sense?—the gabby old woman asked, "Is she expecting you, hon?"

What are you, her doorman?

"Uh, no, I'm surprising her."

The woman's mouth pursed, emphasizing the wrinkles around the too-brightly lipsticked lips. Her friendly tone disappeared. "I have a stun-gun. And pepper spray. And I will tase you, bro."

Mari's door swung inward, almost violently and she stared at them both, unsurprised by his presence. "I'm here," she snapped. "Sorry, I was just, uh, drying my hair."

The neighbor smirked. "I didn't hear the hair dryer." Danny had to think about the words, not sure what the woman had said at first, since it had sounded like "heer drar."

Casting the woman a baleful look, Mari grabbed the front of Danny's shirt, dragging him in.

Laughter on his lips, he waited for her to close the door, then asked, "Would she really have tased me?"

"I should have let her," Mari snapped.

Her eyes snapped fire, and her lips were parted as she heaved deep breaths across them. The color was high in her cheeks, her slightly damp hair curling at her nape, and she smelled like sweetly scented soap, all clean and soft and feminine.

She was beautiful. So damned beautiful she took his breath away. And he suspected she didn't even know it.

Danny swallowed, shoved the instinctive reactions to her away and focused on getting her to listen. She'd let him through the door...but that didn't mean she wouldn't shove him back out of it the minute her neighbor disappeared.

Hell, she lived on the third floor. Given her angry expression, he'd be lucky if she decided not to shove him out a window.

"What are you doing here? How did you find out where I live?"

"I got your contact info from the personnel office," he admitted, knowing how bad that sounded.

"I can't believe they'd give you that," she said, sounding slightly stunned.

"Like I said, I need to talk to you about work. Let's call it official business."

Mari thrust a hand through her hair and turned away from him, as if needing time to gather her thoughts. Danny took the opportunity to look around her apartment. It was a little messy, a little cluttered. Papers and books were stacked on one cushion of an oversize couch, and a nearby bookshelf groaned under the weight of thick textbooks and bulging three-ring binders. Competing for the space were a few knickknacks—a pair of ceramic kittens, a frame containing a picture of a smiling teenage girl; another with two young men. Her siblings?

A sliding glass door revealed a small patio. It didn't provide much of a view, but she'd filled it with plants and colorful outdoor furniture. An open laptop sat on a small café table, and he imagined she often worked out there on beautiful days like this one.

He liked getting this glimpse into her home, her life. It said a lot about her—that she wasn't wound up too tight, that she liked being comfortable, that she was well-read and smart. Of course, that he already knew.

"Okay, so what's this official business?" she asked. Then she glanced at his clothes. "You're certainly not dressed for it."

No, he wasn't. He'd worn jeans and a T-shirt today, not his uniform. He'd figured there was no point in waving a red flag at a bull. "Look, can I at least sit down? The brass had a suggestion about your lecture series, and I told them I'd talk to you about it."

Her mouth rounded into an O, and she blinked a few times, as if genuinely surprised. Or maybe—and it could have been wishful thinking on his part—but maybe that had been a flash of disappointment in her expression when she'd realized he really *had* come to talk about work.

Well, at first, anyway. Then he intended to get personal. If she shoved him out the door afterward, well, at least he'd have had his say.

But God, he hoped she didn't shove him out the door. What he most wanted was another chance with her.

A chance to make her understand why he hadn't called, to convince her he'd wanted to—desperately— and then to start over. Sounded like a good plan to him.

Not looking particularly gracious about it, she waved him toward a chair, which faced the cluttered sofa. Danny took a seat, then immediately felt something swatting at his pants leg.

Startled, he shifted sideways, and glanced under the chair to see a furry white-and-gray face peering out at him. A plaintive meow criticized him for having moved his leg out of swatting range.

"Well, hello there. Fierce little guard cat, are you?" he said with a soft laugh. "You're about as welcoming as your owner."

"Ha ha," Mari said with a definite eye roll. "She's not trying to scratch, she's just trying to get you to play with her."

As if to prove that point, the cat suddenly nudged her nose against a small foam ball, rolling it toward Danny's foot, then meowed loudly.

"Catnip?"

Sighing, Mari shook her head. "I think she hung out with the canine crowd when she was at the shelter where I got her, she's forgotten she's a cat. That sounded like a meow, but I'm sure in her mind she thinks it's a woof."

He raised a brow. "Seriously?"

"Yes. Deep down Brionne really thinks she's a dog," Mari explained. "She wants you to play fetch with her."

Surprised, and wanting to see for himself, Danny took the ball and gently rolled it across the room. The cat darted out from under the chair in a flash, pouncing on the ball, scooping it up in her mouth and dashing back with it. She dropped it right on Danny's shoes and looked up at him with an expectant expression…just like a dog.

He let out a deep laugh. "That's great! The best of both pets—you get to play fetch, but don't have to go outside for any middle-of-the-night business."

"Believe me, I think if I did, she'd beeline for the nearest fire plug," Mari admitted, her voice softening, as did her expression when she looked at her obviously beloved feline companion.

That expression hardened when she returned her attention to him. "Now, what is it you want?"

You. Us. A chance. Another night. A thousand of them.

He started with the basics. "One of the deans attended your lecture yesterday, and he had some concerns."

She sighed deeply. "Old guy with one big, gray eyebrow?"

"That'd be him." Danny quickly explained Riddick's concerns. He emphasized that the man's problems had nothing to do with Mari personally, and were just par for the course with him.

"So he thinks I shouldn't be allowed to be alone with the students? What does he think I'm going to do to them?" she asked, sounding both horrified and embarrassed.

"I think his concerns were for you, rather than about you."

She rolled her eyes. "As if I can't handle a roomful of twenty-year-olds? Good grief."

"Well, I guess because he knows you're not technically a teacher and have no previous experience…"

She nibbled her lip, not arguing the point.

"Here's the thing, though. Apparently the students

who attended the lecture really enjoyed it when I came up and the two of us were interacting. Word got back to the Deputy to the Commandant."

She groaned and lifted a hand to her eyes. "I can't believe I let you distract me. Why on earth did you just show up in the room and ambush me like that?"

"I didn't mean to ambush you," he explained. "I just wanted to see you again."

She huffed. "Sure."

"I mean it, Mari…"

"Why don't you get back to the subject at hand? What, exactly, did the student rumor mill have to say about our verbal sparring match?"

He liked that—a verbal sparring match. That kind of described what they'd done, and actually what he and Mari had been doing since day one. That was one thing he liked best about her—she could talk. She had real conversation skills and a quick wit. There wasn't a lot of calculation or intentional silence or mind games. With Mari, what he'd seen had been what he got.

He just wanted to get more. A lot more.

"Actually, the feedback was very positive. In fact, the students seemed really jazzed up about having a point-counterpoint, he-said/she-said kind of experience. Given Dean Riddick's concerns, and the positive feedback about the two of us, uh…"

She was already shaking her head. "No way."

"'Fraid so. The big boss liked the sound of it so much, he asked me to see if you would agree to make it an ongoing thing.

She shot straight up in her seat, her mouth opening in dismay. "You…he…"

"Yeah. He wants us to work together."

Knowing she had to be feeling not only annoyed, but

perhaps a bit vulnerable about how she'd done—since he remembered how important the job was to her—he quickly explained. "It's not that he thinks you didn't do a great job. In fact, the students *loved* you."

A little too much, in Danny's opinion. He suspected there had been some serious locker room chatter about the hot new teacher on campus, which he didn't like one damned bit. Though he trusted her and knew she could do the job, if his presence in the classroom kept the students eyes in their head and their suggestive remarks behind their teeth, he was all for it.

Besides, even though Riddick was a dinosaur, he wasn't the only campus official who had some pretty old-fashioned ideas. The USNA hadn't gone coed long enough ago for there not to be some remnants of sexism left behind. He didn't like it, tried to combat it when he saw it, but it still appeared on occasion.

"I don't understand," she said with a frown. "What would be the point of us teaming up? Why does he think this would be a good idea?"

"Maybe it's because I'm a living example of what their future might look like," he offered. "I've walked the walk, now I can talk the talk."

"But aren't they already your students?" She rolled her eyes. "They seemed to know you."

"Some of them are. But believe me, my aeronautics class isn't giving them a chance to see me as a person the way your lectures would."

Mari rose from her seat, pacing back and forth across the small room, her arms wrapped tightly around her body. Mumbling under her breath, she admitted, "Things did improve after you got there."

"Had they been discourteous?" he asked with a frown.

"No, not at all. Nothing but respectful, for the most part. But they seemed more lively—more involved—once you got there."

"I'm an ice-breaker. One of *them*. My presence might make them more willing to open up and listen, or even to talk."

She stopped pacing and stared at him. "Which would be a good thing. Some of those kids seem pretty clueless. I think a few of them came to Annapolis without really understanding that it's not all a snazzy uniform, travel and exotic hookers in different ports of call."

He gawked.

"Not that they put it exactly like that," she admitted, her face pinkening.

"Well, they're right about the uniform, and the travel," he said. "But even the newest middie should realize exotic hookers are a surefire way to risk having body parts rot and fall off."

She chuckled a little. It was something, anyway.

Then, as if remembering she wasn't supposed to enjoy being around him—God, she really had her back up about him not calling—her humor disappeared. "I already have the rest of the lectures written, the course series completely laid out."

He held up both hands, palms out. "And I wouldn't interfere with that. I'll sit quietly and listen, then jump in during the discussion period. All right?"

She snagged her bottom lip with her teeth, her thoughts racing across her face in a visible picture of uncertainty. He knew what she was thinking, why she was unsure, and wished he'd started this conversation differently. It wasn't just having to work with someone else that was bothering her. It was having to work with *him*.

Hopefully that wouldn't be an issue once they got to the second reason for his visit. He'd considered having that conversation first, because getting them on even footing personally might have made this professional thing easier. But there had been that slamming-the-door-in-his-face thing to consider. He might never have gotten her to talk to him at all without playing the work card.

Finally, after a long, silent moment of thought, she began to nod, whether in actual agreement or simple acceptance, he couldn't be sure. "Okay," she muttered. "I guess we'll give it a try."

Danny had to smile. Business done with—the official part of his visit was over. Now it was time to move on with the personal part.

He only hoped he could get her to listen to him about what truly mattered, what had really driven him up here this evening.

Them.

THOUGH SHE'D MANAGED to keep up a good front—at least, so she hoped—Marissa wasn't nearly as calm about Danny being here, in her apartment, as she let on. Not only because he had stunned her by showing up. Not just because he was so big and masculine he seemed to suck up all the air in the room. Not even because he looked so damned good to her that she wanted to drink him up like a parched woman offered a glass of cold, refreshing spring water.

No. There was also the little matter of her alter ego.

Mad-Mari. Or, recently, Very *Mad* Mad-Mari.

She'd been sitting out on the balcony writing a blog entry when he'd first knocked. Once she'd realized she would have to answer, or risk her nosy neighbor inviting him in for tea—or macing him!—she'd logged off the site. She'd also quickly closed the door to the hall closet. Inside it were stacks of cartons containing copies of her two books.

The last thing she wanted to do was explain about her alter ego, Mad-Mari.

The irony didn't escape her, nor did the uncomfortable twinge that she was being a little hypocritical. She'd been angry at him for keeping his identity as a navy officer a secret, but now she was keeping a secret of her own. The difference was, he'd *known* she didn't want anything to do with anybody in the military even before they'd slept together, whether he realized that included him or not. But Danny had never come out and said he didn't want to get involved with anybody who wrote, or a blogger.

Quibbling maybe. But still, blogging and writing weren't what she did anymore. They were an amusing pastime. She'd been nothing but honest with him about who she really was and what she really wanted to do.

Besides, it doesn't matter anyway—you're not involved with him.

Right. And they wouldn't be involved in anything but a professional capacity from here on out.

Honestly, though, it wasn't her secret writing life she didn't want him to know about—she wasn't ashamed of it and suspected he'd be amused by her books, as most men with a smidgeon of self-confidence were. Nor did she mind him knowing that she was a semi-famous internet personality.

But the content of her blog had been pretty revealing over the past couple of weeks.

Marissa wasn't ashamed of what she'd written, and she hadn't said a thing that wasn't true—or that she hadn't believed was true at the time. But she'd been pretty open about her heartache. The last thing she wanted was the guy who'd caused it to read all about those long, painful days when she'd waited to hear from him. And how she'd reacted when she hadn't. She'd had a regular bitch session about him with the cyber world, rather than with a few girlfriends over a pitcher of margaritas. Of course, she'd never named him, but he'd know full well who she'd been talking about.

Mr. Perfect. Huh.

She could go back and ditch those entries, she supposed. But she had never played the cyber game that way, and didn't like people who did. It was cowardly—if you couldn't stand behind what you wrote online, you shouldn't write it. Just like you shouldn't say something behind somebody's back that you wouldn't say to their face.

Though, being perfectly honest, she doubted she'd be calling Lieutenant Commander Danny Wilkes a scumsucking user to his face, the way she had on her blog. Well, not in so many words.

Still, she wouldn't delete her pain-filled words, that was a cop-out. She was not, however, going to make it easy for him to stumble across them.

"So," Danny said, breaking the silence that had fallen between them. "Maybe you should tell me the topic of tomorrow's lecture."

"Safe sex," she replied absently.

He coughed into his fist. "Uh…seriously?"

Seeing his wide-eyed expression, she wished she'd come up with a different answer. Talking about sex with Danny wasn't good for her peace of mind. Thinking about having sex with Danny *definitely* wasn't good for her peace of mind.

She should know—she'd thought about it a *lot* over the past couple of weeks. That heated night had imprinted itself on every cell of her brain, the memories of it reaching out to taunt her in quiet moments. Or not-so-quiet ones. Hell, when she'd been grocery shopping last week, she'd had a serious flashback right in the middle of the produce section because she'd squeezed a pair of kiwis to see if they were ripe.

She'd avoided the cucumbers.

And the zucchini.

"Mari, you're seriously going to be talking to a bunch of young sailors about sex?"

Cursing herself for deciding to be bold enough to go for the tough stuff in her second lecture, she replied, "Yes." Mari channeled her inner professor and ignored the lustful free spirit to add, "I intend to go over some of those statistics on body-parts-falling-off, staying safe, that type of thing. Pregnancy rates, how male-female customs in other countries can trip them up. Even immigration issues that could arise if they impregnate a woman while overseas."

"Sounds interesting," he said. "I'm glad I'm going to be there."

She wasn't. "I'm sure it'll be a bore for somebody with your...experience."

He whistled at the insult.

That had been bitchy, and she knew it. Stammering, she explained, "I mean, you've been all over the world, I have no doubt."

Nodding, though he didn't look like he quite believed her, he explained, "That's true. But I meant, I'm glad I'll be there because the kids can be rowdy and you're opening a pretty dangerous door."

"I am perfectly qualified to talk about sex," she said, keeping her tone cool and professional. She only hoped she could maintain it. The longer he stayed here, the harder it was becoming. "I don't need a babysitter."

"I didn't say you did. But I'm glad I'll be there, just in case." Leaning back in the chair and lacing his fingers behind his head, he asked, "So, are you gonna caution them against hooking up with strangers they only met a couple of hours ago?" His expression remained pleasant, his voice holding only a hint of humor.

"Oh, absolutely," she replied quickly. "I intend to preach to them about how *stupid* it is to do something like that. And how, if you do make that mistake once, you'd better make damn sure you don't do it again. You know, learn from your mistakes and all that."

"Mistake, huh?"

"Yes," she replied, her chin going up. "It was a mistake. A lapse in judgment."

He rose to his feet, his smile faltering, as if she'd hurt him a little, if that were possible. "Don't say that yet, okay? You didn't misjudge me. I *am* the guy you met that day, Mari."

Sure. Except for the uniform. And the part where he'd acted as though what had happened had meaning—his tenderness and promises had implied it, even if he hadn't voiced it out loud.

Then there was that promise to call.

Assuming he was ready to leave now that he'd gotten her agreement on the joint lectures, Mari rose, too. She was determined to quietly escort him to the door and not throw her arms around his neck and ask him to do that amazing little move with his hips that he'd used on her that night on his boat.

Good God.

Instead of heading for the door, though, Danny eyed her for a minute, then reached into his back pocket.

Drawing out a sheath of papers, he handed it to her. "Here."

Marissa stared at the pages like he was offering her an unwanted subpoena. "What's that?"

"Just look at them, please," he urged quietly.

Taking one deep, slow breath, then letting it out, Marissa reached for the pages, being careful not to allow her fingers to brush against his. It was bad enough that she was sharing his airspace, she did not need any skin-on-skin contact to mess with her head. Having Danny here—seeing him sitting on that chair, framed against that window, filling the small apartment with that scent—was already doing a number on her.

She glanced at the first page, seeing a photocopy of a receipt from an electronics shop. "So?"

Stepping closer—*too close, don't get so close*—he tapped the neatly manicured tip of his finger on the description of the purchase.

"Congratulations. 3G?"

Ignoring her sarcasm, he pointed to the upper part of the receipt—the date. "I bought it two weeks ago."

"Looks like you got a good deal," she said, pushing the paper toward him.

He wouldn't take it. "Want to know why I bought a new cell phone?"

"'Cause somebody asked, 'Can you hear me now?' and you couldn't?"

He grinned. "No, because I dropped mine in the bay."

She gaped, then muttered, "Gee, I hope nobody ever gives you a bomb to hold."

"Want to know when I dropped it?"

"Not particularly, but I suppose you're going to tell me, anyway."

"About an hour after you left that morning," he explained, stepping even closer, so his pants brushed her calves, bared beneath the capri pants she wore. The contact electrified her...his words even more so.

Because she suddenly remembered what else had happened that morning. How he'd given her his phone to input her number.

He hadn't written it down, hadn't committed it to memory. The *only* way he would have been able to find it was in that phone.

"So you're telling me you lost my number?" she asked, trying to sound flippant, as if she didn't really care. But she did. Oh, did she ever.

"Yes. That's what I'm telling you," he said, his tone steady, unwavering, as if he was trying to convince her with more than mere words. The warmth of his expression aided his endeavor and she found herself softening.

But she quickly steeled herself against it. "Yeah, and nobody knows how to use a phone book anymore."

"I didn't know your last name," he countered.

Hell. He was right. She hadn't learned his that day, either. How insane was that? She'd shared the most wonderfully erotic night with the man and knew exactly the sweet, deep groan he made when he came, but she hadn't found out his last name.

Or his rank. Oy.

"Besides which," he added, "once I did find out your last name—because of a flyer about your speeches on campus—I went searching and found out you're unlisted."

"Oh," she whispered, remembering that. She'd had a few obnoxious letters after her first book came out, and had tried to put up a wall between herself and any overzealous—or overly angry—readers.

"I was tempted to drive around Baltimore to see if I spotted your car parked on the street. I remembered you said you lived near the harbor."

"I park in a private lot," she whispered, a warm, funny feeling rising inside her.

He'd tried to find her? Really? She hadn't been used and then ditched?

"Now, on to Exhibit B."

He pulled the top sheet of paper away, revealing the one below it, which she recognized as a printout of her excerpted dissertation. "After I found out your last name, and hunted for you, I found this article." He tapped the last paragraph on the page. "As you can see, no 'contact the author' section. No URL, no email address, no P.O. Box. Nothing."

Swallowing, she admitted, "I try to maintain my privacy online."

"Yeah, well, I'm sure that's smart, keeping the cyber-stalkers away. Unfortunately, it kept me away, too, and I'm no stalker."

She managed a faint smile. "You never did throw those nails down in the parking lot."

"Nor did I look at your car registration—and see your address—when I was working on your car. Believe me, I've kicked myself for that a dozen times."

He revealed the next sheet in the pile. At first glance, it looked like the printout of an email. It was dated a week ago. "As you can see, I even wrote to the editor of the journal and asked for contact information on the inimitable Marissa Marshall, PhD."

The email confirmed it.

"Not once," he added, pulling the first printout away

to reveal another one…and then another. "Several times. But I got absolutely nowhere."

Mari, whose heart had been thudding wildly from the moment she'd realized the implication of him losing his phone, could only stare, reading the words repeated in his three emails. They confirmed what he'd said—he had definitely been trying to find her. Trying *hard* to find her.

It was true. Danny Wilkes hadn't intentionally blown her off at all. He'd been the victim of a slippery electronic device and Marissa's own need to carefully maintain her privacy.

"You really tried," she whispered.

"Hell, yes," he said, tossing the pages onto the cluttered coffee table. "Even after I'd decided to let fate handle bringing you back into my life, the way fate brought you there the first time, I still gave it my all."

Fate bringing them together. What a romantic concept, not something she'd expect to hear from a military man. Then again, Danny was like no man, military or otherwise, that she'd ever met. He was funny and good-natured, kind, smart, self-deprecating.

Mr. Perfect.

But not, she had to remind herself, Mr. Perfect-For-Her.

How could he be when he was heading down a life-long road she'd sworn to stay away from? Their paths had crossed that one magical, wonderful night…but that was all they could have. Any more might be delicious and wonderful and incredibly pleasureful. But in the end, it would go nowhere. They'd walk in circles, coming back to the center: he was a navy man all the way, and she wanted nothing to do with that lifestyle ever again.

No, Danny was nothing like her father, she knew that

already. Nor was she weak and easily swayed like her mother. But that wasn't the only issue. Even without her parents' lousy example, she knew what that life was like, and she didn't want it. She had no interest in moving all around the globe, at the whim of the military. She wanted to always feel she had a firm foundation beneath her feet, not like her world could be toppled on end with one painful phone call or telegram, or even a simple station-change order. She'd never want any child of hers to have to go to bed at night wondering if Daddy was ever coming home; nor did she want them to have to go to five different schools in a six-year period.

Sleeping with him is not the same as having kids with him.

No, of course it wasn't. But she was pushing thirty and she'd already decided to change her life, to move into a solely mature, adult phase of it. So there could be no backsliding by hooking up with a man with whom she had absolutely no future.

And they had none. She mentally repeated that. *She and Danny had absolutely no future.*

So as wonderful as it was to know their shared night had meant something to him, it didn't make her throw her arms around his neck and beg him to take her to dinner. Or to bed.

"I appreciate your showing me all this," she murmured, meaning it. "Truly. And I'm sorry I believed the worst and didn't give you a chance to explain yesterday." She heard the hint of remorse in her own voice, and hoped he did, too. Because it was entirely genuine.

"You're forgiven," he told her, that handsome grin widening his mouth, making those amber eyes crinkle in the good humor she'd come to associate with him. "So, what do you say, can we start over?"

She swallowed hard, stared into his face, tempted. So damned tempted. Then, somehow, she drew the words she needed to say out of a deep well of strength she hadn't even known she possessed.

"No, Danny. I'm sorry, but we can't."

He looked stunned.

"It's probably best for you to leave now."

Tuesday 5/24/11, 10:50 p.m.
www.mad-mari.com/2011/05/24/Nomore

To quote that kid on *South Park*, "I learned something today."

Something big.

I learned that I shouldn't make assumptions about why things happen without knowing all the facts. And that I should trust my gut when I truly think somebody's a good person, rather than letting my own self-doubts and suspicions make me vulnerable to all kinds of mental nay-saying.

I guess my own background makes me a little less trusting than most people—a shrink would probably say I have abandonment issues. Haha. (Inside joke.)

Whatever the case, I'm here to say I was wrong. Majorly wrong. I feel like shit about it, and I've apologized.

But to be honest, I've learned my lesson, and I'm not going to say anything more here. I'm done spilling my emotions in public. It's not healthy and it's not right. Suffice it to say, I made a big mistake about you-know-who.

He is Mr. Perfect.

Just not my Mr. Perfect.

I can't have him, and I know it. I'm trying to be all

mature and smart about this, but I can't deny it hurts like hell.

Whoops. There I go, spilling my emotions again.

Zip it, Mari!

Okay, moving on. Day 2 of the job. And the job has gotten a whole lot tougher since I accepted it.

I only hope I can make it through.

8

DANNY WAS HAVING A HARD time figuring it out.

Last night, Mari had heard him out, accepted his explanation, and his apology, looking both sheepish and very happy that he'd come to explain the situation to her.

Then she'd promptly shown him to the door.

She hadn't been playing hard to get—he'd have sworn that when she asked him to leave, her eyes were bright with moisture, like she was holding back tears. But she'd been firm about it, refusing his offer to go out for a cup of coffee so they could talk a little more, try to figure things out.

In the end, of course, he'd acceded to her request and left. It had been all he could do to walk out, offering her a nod as she gently closed the door in his face. Because what he'd really wanted to do was take her hands in his, sit her down and make her tell him what was really bothering her.

For a second, he'd worried that she was seeing someone else—that he had been the "other man." But there had been no evidence of a guy in that apartment. And he couldn't see her as being someone who'd cheat. Not after the sadness he'd heard in her voice when she'd told him about her parents' bad choices. God, what a tough background.

So, no. He didn't see her being a cheat. Plus, he didn't imagine her neighbor would have kept her big mouth shut about it if another man was regularly showing up at Mari's door.

"So what the hell is it?" he mumbled as he headed for the lecture hall. "What gave you such cold feet?"

Of course the military thing crossed his mind. She'd sounded pretty convincing when talking to her students about some women not being interested in that lifestyle. But hell, they'd already clicked so beautifully, had a real chemistry and connection. He just couldn't imagine the anxiety over something that might or might not happen, far down the road, would make her shut him out of her life now.

He honestly didn't know the truth, but he intended to find out. Fortunately, she had to spend time with him over the next couple of weeks—at least a couple of hours every Monday and Wednesday. Yes, they'd be in front of an audience, but seeing her in public was better than not seeing her at all. And hopefully he'd get her to open up and be honest about what she was thinking.

Danny didn't spend a lot of time evaluating why he'd fallen so hard and so fast for her. Maybe he should have. Maybe he should at least be curious. Maybe a part of him should have been wondering if he'd just been single too long and was seeing the perfect woman in somebody he barely knew.

None of those things were crossing his mind.

Just as he'd always known he needed flight, he had known right away that he needed her. Maybe not forever—he wasn't such a romantic that he believed in love at first sight.

But there was that serendipity element.

Things happen for a reason.

The fact was, she'd come into his life and completely knocked him off his feet—the first time that had happened with any woman. It had to mean something.

"Hey, Midas!" a voice said as he reached the lecture hall. Through the inset glass in the door, he saw the room was already filled to the brim with students. Even more than there had been the other day.

Apparently word had spread about the sexy new lecturer.

"Hey, Quag," he replied, watching as his friend peered through the door, as well.

"She in there?"

He stiffened. He had not told Quag that Marissa—the woman he'd been trying so desperately to find—was the new instructor on campus. "Who?"

"The smoking hot teacher the kids have been talking about."

"I hope you didn't encourage them in that," he replied, his tone steely.

Quag shrugged. "You think I'm stupid? I don't gossip with students. But it's kinda hard not to hear the whispers."

"Yeah, well, next time you hear them whispering, you send 'em my way and I'll give them so much classwork, they'll be too busy to talk smack about a lady."

As if finally realizing Danny was steamed, Quag whistled and then smirked. "*She's* the one? The mystery woman?"

He replied with a brief nod.

Before Danny had to do anything more than frown,

his playboy friend put his hands up, palms out. "Okay, dude, no harm, no foul. Hands off. You saw her first." Then he sauntered off down the hall, whistling as he went.

"I've got an idea. How about you two go out hunting— whoever brings back the biggest mastodon leg gets me. How's that sound?"

Oh, shit.

Danny glanced behind him and saw Marissa standing a few feet away, her expression as glacial as her tone had been. She'd apparently heard every word.

"Hi. I didn't realize you hadn't gone inside yet."

"I had to drop off some paperwork. Now, if you'll excuse me…" she said, trying to push past him to the door.

He put a hand on her arm, not restraining her, but gently asking her to stay. She paused—the briefest hesitation—but it was enough to tell him she wasn't *too* angry.

"I'm sorry," he said. "I'm not a caveman, I promise. Quag's just a little over-the-top."

"Let me guess, another flyboy?"

"Something wrong with flyboys?"

She shook her head and forced a visibly tight smile. "Not a thing. I'm sure you're all very proud of your… wingspans."

"Oh, we are," he murmured. "And don't even ask about how much we love deep dives, tight rolls…all that torque and thrust."

Her throat quivered as she swallowed.

He stepped toward her, and she backed up, step after step, until she'd slipped into the alcove of the next lecture hall down. Unlike hers, this one was empty. No prying eyes could possibly be watching from behind the glass.

They were tucked away, invisible to anyone unless that person walked right by this alcove.

He hadn't intended to corner her here. Neither, however, was he disappointed by that fact.

"I shouldn't have left last night without telling you how much I've missed you," he admitted. He lifted a hand, scraping his palm against her upper arm, noting the silkiness of the blouse, remembering the even silkier skin underneath.

"Danny…"

"You've missed me, too," he claimed, knowing it was true.

She caught her bottom lip between her teeth, but didn't try to deny it. The chemistry between them swirled, thickening the air in the tiny space. Every breath he took was filled with her scent, every beat of his heart echoed by Mari's.

"I thought you weren't going to wear your hair like that anymore," he said, moving even closer until his foot slid between her high-heeled shoes.

Mari was again dressed in that so-prim-but-so-sexy style that drove him utterly wild. He wanted to sink his hands into her blond hair and tug it out of that tight, compressing bun. Wanted to kiss the swollen redness back into her lips, to tear open the simple white blouse, not caring if every button went flying.

He wanted to have her. Here. Now.

Funny, he suspected he wanted her more right at this minute than he had last night, when they'd been alone in her apartment and could actually have done something about it.

Damn, he really was hot for teacher.

"Stop," she ordered weakly.

"You stop."

"Stop what?"

"Stop pretending you don't want me, too."

She licked her lips, sucked in an audible breath, then tilted her head to look up at him. "I'm not *pretending* I don't want you."

His heart fell. Was he really so far off base? Was he really misreading that smokiness in her eyes, the husky quality of her voice? Had he imagined that flick of her pretty pink tongue against her lips as she stared at his mouth, as if she'd been thinking of nothing but kissing him since the first word they'd exchanged?

No. He hadn't. He knew he hadn't.

"I have to hand it to you, sweetheart. You are one beautiful liar."

Then he proved it to her. Proved she was lying.

Proved she wanted him.

Needing to taste her or die, he dropped his hands to her hips and tugged her close, until the warmth of her thighs melted against his. He didn't give her a chance to think twice, merely bending to capture her mouth in a kiss that went from Rated G to Rated X in about 2.9 seconds flat.

She parted her lips for him instantly, accepting his kiss and giving it right back. Her sweet, warm tongue thrust against his own—deeper, hotter—and he could hear the helpless little whimpers of pleasure in her throat.

Lifting her hands, Mari twined her fingers in his hair, arching against him. Her breasts pressed against his chest, the points of her nipples stabbing him as her arousal grew.

He felt her slim thighs part, then one rose against the outside of his leg as she arched toward him, so her warmth cupped his hardening cock. It was frustrating as hell through their clothes—but felt so good. So god-damned good.

A door slammed nearby, and he reluctantly ended the kiss, managing a small step back. They both heaved in a few breaths. He wondered if she had any idea how beautiful she looked when she'd been well and truly kissed.

Well. And truly. He almost smiled, the echo of her words from that morning on the boat replaying in his mind.

He wanted a repeat of that morning. And definitely a repeat of the preceding night.

"I wasn't lying. I'm not pretending not to want you, Danny, because I *do* want you, and I freely admit it," she told him, her voice thick. As though she just couldn't help herself.

Danny couldn't prevent a tiny, triumphant smile. God, it was good to hear those words come out of her mouth. He wanted to taste them on her lips before they stopped echoing in his ears. Wanted to drag her into the nearest private room with a locking door and do a whole hell of a lot more than kiss her. What he most wanted was to pick up right where they'd left off seventeen days and two hours ago.

"But I'm not going to let myself have you," she said, that prim teacher's tone coming back.

All his visual fantasies disappeared like a bubble pricked with a pin. Thrusting a frustrated hand through his hair, Danny took a step back. "Just tell me why. You said you understood about the phone, that you believed me…"

"I do believe you." Then, with an almost sad little shake of her head, she finally admitted the truth. "But I just don't want a guy in uniform. Period. End of story. I thought I made that pretty clear."

Though he'd considered the possibility, he was still surprised by her words. Long-term was one thing, okay, he could buy that. But it seemed downright crazy to insist they couldn't indulge in the hot sex they both craved just because of his damn job.

"You're willing to forego the guy just because of the clothes on his back?"

Her lips trembled, revealing that hint of vulnerability again. Then she slowly nodded. "Yes. I am."

He tried a self-deprecating smile. "Hey, it's not like I proposed. Can't you bend your rule and hang out with me?"

She rolled her eyes. "Hang out? I think you mean make out."

"That's so high school. What I mean is have hot, steamy, can't-get-it-out-of-your-head sex."

She muttered a curse word under her breath, and he saw the way her nipples drew to even tighter points under her blouse.

She didn't want to want him.

But oh, she definitely *did* want him.

"Come on, Mari. Let's have a fling."

She nibbled her lip, her flushed face revealing more than words ever could about what she was thinking.

"Come home with me tonight."

She gulped and slowly shook her head.

Danny scraped a tiny strand of hair that had come loose from her bun off her cheek, trailing his fingertips over her soft skin. "You don't have to fall in love with me," he whispered. "Just be my lover."

"Fall in love with you…" she whispered, shaking her head slowly. Then, blinking a few times, as if to clear her mind, she said, "No. I'm sorry, Danny. It's just not going to happen. I might desire you, but I don't want to sleep with you again."

SHE SO TOTALLY WANTED to sleep with that man again.

Mari had absolutely no doubt about it. Every fiber of her being demanded that right—that privilege. One night out of a lifetime was just not enough to spend in the arms of a man like Danny. It would be against the laws of nature for her not to want to spend another night in his arms. And unless she remained very strong, she probably would.

It had taken her all but ten minutes to figure that out. She'd made her confident claim, swept past him into the classroom, started delivering her talk—about sex—and promptly forgotten every little reason she'd had for turning him down.

Because he was impossible to resist. Even sitting quietly in the corner of the room, out of her line of vision, she was intensely aware of his presence. She felt the heat of his stare on her, heard the occasional deep, masculine chuckle, could swear she could feel the warmth of his breaths if she stepped within a few feet of him.

Oh, hell, yes, she probably *was* going to sleep with him again.

And she'd been insane to pretend she wouldn't.

But she'd only sleep with him. Only have an affair with him. She'd only take him as a lover…not as her love.

Because loving him was the one thing she just couldn't allow. Loving Danny Wilkes just didn't fit in with her plans for the rest of her life.

All those thoughts raced through her mind while she delivered her prepared remarks. Fortunately, she had a hard copy of her entire speech and was able to read most of it, because heaven knew, if she'd gotten off track, she might never have found her way back. She'd always been a multitasker, and was able to sail through to the end without revealing the lustful thoughts filling her mind.

Or so she thought.

Now, though, she had to wonder. Because when she finished and saw the rather blank looks on the faces of the students, she wondered if she'd screwed up somehow.

"Uh, are there any questions?" she asked.

Silence.

The young men looked at each other. From behind her, she heard Danny clear his throat. She glanced in his direction, and realized he was staring at her with something that looked a little like shock on his face.

Oh, hell. What had she said? What in the name of *heaven* had she said?

"Uh, yeah, I have a question," said a young man standing near the back of the room. He waved his hand to get her attention, smiling brightly when their eyes met. "Did you seriously just tell all of us that while we should always have safe sex, and be prepared, there's absolutely nothing wrong with an occasional booty call?"

Had she said that? She hadn't said that. No. Definitely not. *Please, God, let me not have said that.*

"Uh, can I answer that, Dr. Marshall?" Danny asked, rising from his seat and approaching the lectern.

"Oh, please," she whispered, thinking frantically, grabbing for her notes and wondering what on earth she'd done. Had she written buddy and said booty? Had she meant to talk about Tail*hook* and mentioned hooking up?

"I think what Dr. Marshall was *trying* to say," Danny

explained to the wide-eyed, titillated-looking students, "is that while everybody can get carried away and have sexual affairs you might not have intended to have, you can never forget to protect yourself."

Sure. Right. That's what she'd meant. The one kid had just misunderstood.

"That's not what she said," another boy called.

"Shit," she whispered under her breath.

Danny cast her a quick glance, and she'd swear merriment danced in those bewitching eyes of his. Then he turned his focus on the boys, all of whom looked a whole lot more interested in her topic of discussion now than they had when she'd first started speaking.

The first student—who looked about eighteen, with a smug face and big, knowing smirk—spoke again. "She said sometimes you just gotta do it—have sex, even if you know it's never gonna go anywhere else. Which, dude, don't get me wrong, sounds totally all right with me. But it's not exactly what I expected to hear from a teacher *here*."

Danny shrugged. "You're human. You're male. The drive is natural. You almost certainly like sex—or you will like it, someday."

Right. Like any of these sailor-boys hadn't been getting ass thrown at them left right and center since they'd first flashed around their acceptance letters to the academy.

"So she's saying we should just go for it, if it's offered? Get it from anybody who'll give it up?"

"No!" Marissa yelped, hurrying back over to the podium, her heels clicking like little popgun shots on the tile floor. "That's definitely not what I was saying." She gave Danny a pleading expression, begging him to back her up. "I'm saying…you're human. You have urges. It's understandable. But you don't want to get hurt, or hurt someone else."

"Save it for health class," someone muttered, to a smattering of laughter.

"I'm not just talking about STDs," she insisted, finding her footing now, as she felt strongly about this lesson. These kids needed to understand. "I know you're all going to be big tough sailors or SEALs, or…pilots."

"Naval Aviators!" one of the young men clarified.

She glanced at Danny. "Aviators. Sorry. But you still have hearts, which means you can still get them broken."

"By some cheap tramp?"

She cast a hard stare at the student who'd said that. "Maybe not *you*—I doubt you're going to be falling in love anytime soon, because with that attitude, no girl will ever take you seriously enough to let you get close."

The comment was greeted by snickers from the boy's classmates. He flushed a little, then mumbled an apology under his breath. That could have been because he felt bad about it, because she'd embarrassed him…or because Danny had taken one small-but-threatening step in his direction. Mari had seen him, out of the corner of her eye.

So maybe it was a good thing that he was here. At the very least it was making her audience listen.

"The thing is, it's not just a disease you risk when you have meaningless sex with someone. You also risk getting your heart broken."

Danny cleared his throat and murmured, "But aren't some risks worth taking?"

"If you know it's going to end badly, why even start?"

"Because you can't *know* anything of the kind," he replied.

She frowned, refusing to glance at him. "Meaning you've got to be sensible about it. You can't always just do what you *want* to do *when* you want to do it."

"So how about doing it later?" he quipped, drawing laughter from the students.

She didn't think they caught the suggestive undertone of the remark, but she certainly did. "Okay, how about doing it later?" she replied, lifting a brow. "Is there ever a good time for heartache?"

"Is there ever a good time to give up on something that could be spectacular just because the timing's not right?" he countered.

Spectacular. Wow. It had been. And oh, did she like that he thought so, too.

He wasn't finished. "How can you just *decide* you don't have a chance of winning? It's like you're never even picking up the bat to take a swing. That's pretty cowardly."

And to think she'd recently decided she was going to sleep with him again. Right now, she wanted to tape his mouth shut.

Or fill it with something. Hmm...

"Discretion is the better part of valor," she quoted.

"Winners never quit."

"Those who fight and run away..."

"Will get their asses chased to the ends of the earth by the U.S. Navy!"

Every boy in the room laughed and whooped at that one.

"I mean," she said, once they'd quieted again, "sometimes it's better to not take a chance."

"Sorry. Playing it safe—never taking risks—is definitely not something we teach around here."

"We're not talking about warfare."

He grinned at the other males in the room. "Hey, all's fair in love and war, right?"

They again laughed with him. He had a rapport with the boys—they obviously liked him, respected him.

But he was not helping here. Probably because he was talking about them—their personal relationship—while she was talking about…

Them. Their personal relationship.

Damn it, she'd been doing the same thing. Pretending to be imparting some kind of lesson when, in reality, she'd been sending him a message about why she'd turned him down, why she shouldn't change her mind.

Of course, considering she'd *already* pretty well changed her mind, she had to wonder why she bothered making the effort.

"I suppose you could go into that kind of relationship with your guard up, expecting nothing, not allowing yourself to feel anything." Seeing the way his brow drew lower over his eyes, she added, "Don't you go into battle that way?"

"We go in expecting to triumph," he told her. "Thoughts of defeat don't ever enter our minds."

"Lucky you."

"I promise you, it's really not that hard," he murmured.

She tore her gaze off his face, which had suddenly softened with tenderness, as if he wanted to tell her she was wrong, that she should expect they could make it. They could win in this crazy romantic-sexual game they'd been playing since the moment they'd met.

But she just didn't buy it. Not in the long run.

Addressing the boys, she added, "But it doesn't work that way. Not for everybody. So is that really wise? Is it worth doing it if you're not going into it with your whole heart?"

A student whooped. "Hells yeah, it's worth it! Long as I'm going into it with my whole..."

"Watch it!" Danny snapped, frowning and pointing an index finger at the kid.

The boy, obviously used to bragging around his pals, bit his lip and stared at Marissa. "Sorry, ma'am."

"It's all right," she replied. "And on that note, I think we're out of time."

A few groans said the students weren't necessarily ready to end this conversation. But Marissa was. Most definitely.

Smiling at the boys who stopped by to thank her, she quickly turned her attention back to her notes. Next time, she was going to have to print them in a huge font, and study them intently before she walked through the door of the classroom.

Not getting the taste kissed out of her mouth by Danny Wilkes right before a lecture would probably be a good idea, too.

"So, got anything you want to talk about?" he asked once they were alone in the room.

"Nope."

"Those certainly were some interesting remarks."

"I didn't actually say..."

"Yeah, you did."

"Hell."

"If it's any consolation, I think it made the boys like you more. You have street cred—they think you're real."

"A real blithering idiot," she mumbled.

"You didn't blither at all. Huh. Blither, is that a real word?"

"I have no idea. And thanks."

"Hey, I'm serious. You might not have been reading off your notes, but everything you said makes sense."

He stepped closer, filling all the airspace around her. She should tell him not to invade her personal bubble like that—she couldn't think when he did. But somehow, she couldn't manage it.

It simply felt too good to be close to him.

"I'm impressed. *Doctor* Marshall."

She managed a slight step back, mindful of the fact that chattering students were walking by in the hall, right outside the closed door. "Well, you didn't help much."

"Aww, I'm crushed. I thought I did great. Got them to believe you didn't really say what they thought you said…"

"Thanks," she said, unable to prevent a tiny grin. He was just so full of life, self-confidence, good humor. "Now, I really should go."

"Got a wake to get ready for?"

She lifted a curious brow.

"I mean, you know, since you're always planning for the bad stuff. Heartbreak, loneliness…you probably help plan funerals in your spare time, right?"

She couldn't prevent laughter from bursting from her mouth. "Anybody ever tell you you're an ass?"

"Anybody ever tell you you've got a great ass?"

She smirked. "More times than I can count."

"Sassy wench."

"Damn it, Danny, stop making me like you."

Shrugging, he replied, "Can't help it. You just do. The same way I can't help liking you."

"I'm trying not to, believe me."

"Yeah, what's with that?" he asked, sounding genuinely confused. "I mean, okay, I can get being self-protective. I know your background left you pretty mistrusting of guys in uniform. But you put up barriers to something as simple as friendship like nobody I've ever known."

"Friendship? That's what we've been talking about here?"

"Hell, no," he said, flashing those dimples. "But it's a start."

A start…definitely the start of something. She suspected that something could be pretty wonderful.

If only he were that simple blue-collar mechanic she'd thought him to be on the day they'd met. Then she'd jump into this with both feet first, without hesitation.

It was still tempting to jump, but she was hesitating. How crazy was she to start down the road on a trip she couldn't finish? She only needed to go back and read her own blog entries during those two long weeks when she hadn't heard from him to remember how deeply this man affected her. So what kind of crazy woman would set herself up for more of the same?

"I don't suppose your tour of duty's almost up, is it?"

He met her gaze steadily, the smile fading. Serious, intent, he replied, "No, it's not, but I might not always be doing what I'm doing now. I can, however, say with near certainty that I don't see myself becoming a civilian again anytime soon. If you can't handle that…"

"I've already told you I can't handle that!"

"Can't, or won't?"

Good point.

"How about this. Get rid of the can't. Get rid of the won't. And for now, let's leave it at might."

Might? A simple word, but it bore such a wealth of possibilities. So many different outcomes, so many variables. It could lead to sadness, disappointment and regret. Or it could lead to incredible happiness.

And *mightn't* she live to regret it if she said no?

Thinking it over, she finally met his steady stare and replied, "Okay, Danny. I *might* be able to do that."

He smiled, moved closer, lifted a hand to her face. She curled her cheek into the warm, rough fingers, melting a little. That kiss before class had filled her mind with all kinds of wicked ideas, and she wanted another one. Now. Right now.

But there was that unlocked door…

"Hold that thought," he told her.

"What thought?"

"The thought that you want me to kiss you again."

She didn't deny it, smiling as she watched him jog to the doorway and flick the lock. The chattering from out in the hallways had lowered significantly. Eyeing the clock and seeing it was lunchtime, she figured the students had all headed outside to enjoy the day. The building was rapidly growing as quiet as a tomb.

He turned back to face her. Their stares met and held for a long moment. Marissa's heart was pounding so hard in her chest, she wondered if he heard it. Because he had that look in his eye. That sexy, I-want-you look. The one with which she'd become so familiar during the long passionate night they'd shared.

She licked her lips, remembering. Anticipating.

As if that tiny movement had broken any last bonds of restraint, Danny strode back toward her, eating up the floor in three long strides. Without saying a word, he stepped right up to her, sweeping his arms around her and capturing her mouth with his own.

"Mmm," she groaned, parting her lips, wanting that warm, seeking tongue. Wanting the heat, the connection, the intimacy.

She lifted her arms around his neck, tugging him even closer, tilting her head to the side and inviting him to do more. So much more. Starting with pleasing her, of course, but ending with filling up the emptiness and driving away the remnants of sadness and regret she'd felt during the two weeks she'd thought she would never see him again.

His mouth tasted sweet and intoxicating, his breath mingling with hers, sending a rush of warmth down into her lungs every time she inhaled. Their tongues mated and danced, with gentle thrusts and deep tastes, the rhythm of the kiss matching the natural one between their bodies as they began to sway into one another, mimicking the deeper connection yet to come.

It was crazy. They were in a public building, a place where they both worked. If they were going to do this, last night in her apartment would have been the prime opportunity.

But she had been stupid last night. Stupid and cowardly.

Now she was brave and hungry. So hungry she wanted to gobble him up.

Without saying a word, Marissa began to take tiny steps backward, toward the front corner of the room... out of the line of sight of that window in the door. He followed her lead, not letting their mouths part, the kiss becoming almost more frantic. Desperation and lust were overwhelming them and for the life of her, she simply didn't care.

Once her back hit the wall and she could go no farther, she said, "This is madness, you know."

"I know."

He reached up into her hair and began pulling out the bobby pins holding it up. As the strands fell, he twined them in his fingers. Then those perfect, wonderful hands moved down, caressing her neck, landing on her shoulders.

Mari arched toward his touch, her breasts aching. Her nipples had hardened into hard little points, overflowing with sensation, and the need to feel his hands on her—his mouth—had her shivering down to her toes. So when he ended the kiss and moved his lips down her throat, tasting his way down to the top hem of her modest blouse, she could only groan her approval.

"I know other guys might think tight, sexy clothes are hot, but for the rest of my life, I'm gonna get hard when I even think about you in a prim little blouse."

She pressed against him, feeling proof that he was already there. *So there.* Unable to resist, she reached down, cupping that thick ridge of flesh through his pants.

He grabbed her hand, lifted it over her head and pressed it against the wall with a deep, helpless growl. "Huh-uh."

She liked that she drove him so crazy. Liked even more that he was being so sweetly aggressive, holding her in place, pinning her against the wall as if he wouldn't let her go if somebody held a gun to his head. But not hurting her. She knew he would never do that.

"Don't move," he warned, the throaty need in his voice thrilling her. "Just *let* me."

Let him. He didn't specify what she was supposed to let him do, but frankly, she didn't give a damn. Because right now, she was ready to let him do anything he wanted to her.

She gave her assent with a gentle moan of pleasure as

he moved his hands to her blouse and began unbuttoning it. His fingers were shaking, as if he feared he'd go too fast and tear something. Which she honestly wouldn't mind…except for the fact that they had to get out of this room sooner or later.

The cool air rushed against each inch of skin as he bared it, and she quivered, wanting him to warm her with his big, strong hands, his amazing mouth.

He laughed softly, as if hearing her silent plea, but didn't give her what she wanted. Instead, as he tugged the blouse free of her skirt, he dropped to his knees, kissing her stomach just above her waistband.

"Danny," she whispered, twining her fingers in his thick hair.

"You smell good," he told her, inhaling deeply. Whether he meant her body lotion or her body, she didn't know. But she had a feeling…

He reached around her, squeezing her bottom lightly, then finding the tiny zipper. Tugging it down, he whispered, "Wearing anything underneath today?"

"See for yourself."

The skirt fell. And he saw. "I like," he growled.

Something—perhaps a deep, inner instinct that had known this was inevitable—had made her grab her tiniest, sexiest pair of black panties this morning. They didn't cover much—just a triangle of fabric rested over the thatch of curls covering her sex.

As the skirt puddled around her feet, Danny slid his big hands down, stroking her hips, encircling her bare thighs. Then, as if unable to resist, he tugged her closer, until his lips scraped the black fabric. She whimpered, feeling his warm breath, remembering the feel of his tongue. Every inch of her that wasn't already soft and wet got that way pronto and the anticipation of him licking into her softness had her panting, on the verge of begging.

He didn't do what she was dying for, though. Didn't flick that tongue out for a taste. "I want to bury my face here," he whispered. "I want to drink from you. But that might be kinda hard to hide."

Hell. He was right. It wasn't like he could cover his face and hide the fact that he smelled of earthy, elemental woman.

"Later," he promised.

"Right back at you," she assured him, knowing she wanted the pleasure of taking him into her mouth again.

Though a little frustrated at not getting that incredibly wicked, wanton experience right now, she relaxed as he began to kiss his way up her body. Because this was more than okay, too. Her breasts *ached* for his attention, her nipples so hard and taut they almost hurt as they scraped against the fabric of her bra.

Thankfully, when he reached her bra, he didn't hesitate, deftly opening the front fastener with a flick of his fingers. Her breasts spilled free, and he stared for a moment, his eyes gleaming in approval. "Beautiful."

"Please," she whispered, arching toward him, silently telling him what she needed.

He didn't torment her this time, as if he needed that connection just as much. He lifted a hand to one breast, plumping, squeezing lightly, tweaking the nipple. Then he caught it in his mouth and drew deep. No warning, no buildup, just quick, hard sucking that sent her out of her ever-loving mind.

His other hand slipped between her thighs, stroking her damp panties, and the sensations combined to send a fast, hot little orgasm bursting through her.

She shook, took the goodness and the delight of it, but didn't let it deter her from what she really wanted.

Him. Inside her. Now.

As if he knew it, he reached into his pocket and grabbed a condom. This time, he didn't push her hands away when she reached for his pants and quickly unfastened his belt. But her fingers struggled with the zipper—God, he was so damned big—and he pushed them away and finished the job himself. Shoving the pants and his boxer-briefs down his hips, he yanked the condom on that massive erection and pushed her harder against the wall.

"Oh, yes, please," she said, tilting her head back and lifting one leg in welcome. She wrapped it around the back of his thigh, smiling as she felt him tear her panties off and nudge into the wet lips of her sex with the thick tip of his cock. She felt greedy and hungry, wanting it all. She had no trepidation this time, no worries about his size. She was dripping wet and felt totally empty and ready for him.

"Do it, take me," she snapped, wanting him to drive her into the wall. Wanting him slamming into her so hard it hurt.

Danny picked up on her urgency, but, as if worried he might injure her by pressing her harder into the corner, he reached for her bottom and lifted her up off the floor. She immediately wrapped her arms around his neck, and her legs around his lean hips, sinking onto his shaft with a deep cry of delight.

He threw his head back, the cords of muscle in his neck flexing against her hands as he groaned with pleasure. Mari squeezed him, deep inside, gaining a shudder that told her he liked it.

"God, you feel good."

"You *make* me feel good," she replied.

She slowly began to pull away from him, liking being joined, but needing that deep plunge, that helpless frenzy.

He gave her exactly what she needed, holding her bottom tight, drawing out of her, hesitating, then driving home again.

She buried her face in his shoulder, sure her cries would become too loud. And could only hold on tight as he withdrew and then thrust deep. Again. Again. Until thought was gone. Reality was gone. Time, place, past, future.

Gone.

There was just this. Just the heat and the sweat and the intensity and the power.

Just the good.

"Oh, yeah," he groaned, his tone telling her he was close to coming.

"Do it," she ordered. "Come on, Danny, take us there."

His hands dug almost painfully into her hips, and he pushed her into the corner, hard. She was braced against the wall, able to lean back, bettering the angle. And this time when he plunged, he carved out a place for himself deeper in her body than she had ever realized was even possible.

They ground together, the position building her own delight so that she came again, this time long and steady, not a hot flash but a tidal wave of sensation.

Hearing by her cries, or seeing by her expression that she'd been brought to the very highest peak of pleasure, Danny let go of any last restraints. He drove hard, guttural groans emerging from his mouth as he rode them both toward oblivion. Then, finally, with a deep cry of pure satisfaction, he joined her in it.

They panted together for a long minute, her, naked, clinging to him, pressed between his hard, still-clothed body and the wall. She didn't think her legs would support her if she tried to stand. Fortunately, Danny's massive arms and powerful shoulders seemed fully capable of holding her all day if he wanted to.

She hoped he wanted to. Because as far as she was concerned, this had just been the let's-blow-off-some-steam encounter. A long, slow, steamy one was definitely in order.

They still had promises to keep, after all.

"Hey, Mari?" he whispered against her hair.

"Yes?"

His chest rumbled a little as a laugh rose within him.

"Hate to tell you this, sweetheart…but you're going to have to walk out of here without a pair of panties under your skirt again."

She laughed as well, remembering how he'd ripped them off her. "You know, ever since meeting you, Lieutenant Commander Wilkes, I've discovered I kinda like going commando."

9

Friday 5/27/11, 03:30 p.m.
www.mad-mari.com/2011/05/27/TGIF

Sorry my post is late going up today—I've been very, uh, busy for the past couple of days.

Anyway, whoop! It's Friday, meaning, another week over and less deep in debt.

I guess that's a pretty obscure reference. I'm badly paraphrasing an old song my dad used to play when I was a kid. The point is, I've finished my first full (well, part-time) week of gainful employment.

Honestly, I think I did okay. That was despite a few unexpected curveballs. I think I adapted to them pretty well. Actually, I've adapted to a lot of things pretty well.

La-la-la-la-la. (Picture me sticking my fingers in my ears and humming so I don't have to listen to you all beg me to say WHAT things have you adapted to, Mari?)

Never you mind 'bout that.

So, it's Friday. Bad Date Day, remember? Usually I'd ask you to spill the details of your worst date in recent memory. But I'm thinking today we might change things up a bit. Let's be a little more optimistic and upbeat, shall we? How about we share stories of a wonderful date. The most exciting, romantic, memorable date you've ever had. Best story (in my judgment) gets autographed copies of BOTH my books.

Yes, it's still me, Mari. My giddy, romantic teenage sister has not snuck into my place, taken over my computer and posted this mushy stuff. And I have no doubt I'll still manage to find something to snark about in the sweet stories that are about to unfold. But hey, give it a shot, why don't you? We could all use a little romance, right?

Except for me. I've already got my own! (haha—gotcha, didn't I?!)

TTYL—

Mari

P.S. I have a date tomorrow night myself. I so don't remember how to do this dating thing!

Hmm...do people still kiss on the first date?

:bats lashes:

DURING THE REGULAR SCHOOL year, or the official upcoming summer term, Danny would have had very little spare time. Between actually teaching, grading, counseling and hands-on interaction with the students, he'd be working a regular nine-to-five schedule.

Now, though, in the no-man's-land between semesters, he had lots of unclaimed hours on his hands. Which was a very good thing. Because after that wild, passionate encounter with Mari in the classroom, he had taken the next two days off and they'd gone from steamy encounter to seismic event.

The two of them had left campus Wednesday afternoon—somehow managing to avoid running into anyone he knew, who might have noticed his rumpled clothing or her well-kissed mouth—and spent the next forty-eight hours sans clothes. They'd pretty much remained in her bed, getting out of it only to call for Chinese takeout, or to move their steamy sexual play into the shower, or, once, very late Thursday night, out onto her balcony.

They'd probably still be there, if not for the fact that Danny had really needed to go back down to Annapolis Friday afternoon to get some other clothes, and to check his mail. He'd been doing that compulsively, knowing he should be hearing any day about his application to NASA.

That was something he should probably tell Mari about. With her aversion to him being in the navy, he couldn't help but think she'd view it as good news. And as crazy as it was to be thinking long-term when they'd only known each other less than a month, he couldn't deny his thoughts were going in that direction. Every minute he spent with her reinforced his certainty that something pretty special was happening between them. He suspected she felt the same way.

So, yeah, hearing that he might end up leaving the military, living a pretty normal life in Houston rather than being shipped around the world every other year, might appeal to her. A lot.

Frankly, though, he didn't want to talk about it yet. Very few people knew, and he liked it that way, not wanting anyone around him to get their expectations up as high as his were. He had the right stuff, and knew he had a good chance of getting in. But so did a lot of other qualified guys.

By Saturday evening, after more than twenty-four hours away from her, he was more than anxious to head back up to Baltimore. And the closer he got to her place, the more anxious he became. It would be hard not to walk through her front door, swoop her into his arms and carry her straight to bed. He had become insatiable for the woman.

But he would refrain. Tonight, he wanted to take Mari on their first *official* date—her thank-you lunch hadn't really counted, in his opinion. Mainly because she'd paid.

This one, dinner at a nice restaurant, was the real deal. And he wanted it to *be* perfect.

It seemed kinda crazy—the two of them "dating" after the intensely erotic things they'd been doing to each other for the past couple of days. But it was a good kind of crazy. An important kind of crazy. She needed to know he wanted to be with her, not just to be between her legs.

But, oh, had *that* become one of his favorite places on the face of the earth.

Arriving in the city and parking, he called up from the street, knowing she'd be watching for him so he wouldn't have to knock on her door. Her nosy neighbor had kept him talking for almost a half hour the day he'd finally left. And if he again had to see her knowing smirk and accompanying eyebrow wag as she reminded him how *thin* the walls were, he'd lose it. Talk about embarrassing. It was one thing to get some ragging from a buddy, but from a woman who looked like his grandma?

Well, to be honest, she resembled his grandpa more.

Mrs. Faraday wasn't the most attractive old lady he'd ever met.

Unfortunately, the woman had the ears of a six-year-old waiting for Santa on Christmas Eve. He'd no sooner taken one cautious step down the carpeted hallway before her door creaked open.

"Oh, you're back! Can't get enough, huh?"

He managed a tight smile. "Hello, Mrs. Faraday."

"She's in there, hon, she just got out of the shower." She gave him a thumbs-up. "And this time, I heard the hair dryer running. She's obviously getting dolled up for ya."

He grimaced. The woman obviously hadn't been kidding about those thin walls. He couldn't imagine how much her ears must have been burning Wednesday night. Christ, Danny's own throat had been sore from all the groaning. And he couldn't imagine how Mari's felt…the woman was a screamer.

Don't think about that. Not if he wanted to get past this eagle-eyed old woman with his dignity intact. Because if her vision was as good as her hearing, she'd surely noticed if he tented his trousers.

"I don't suppose you're any good with your hands, are you, hon?" she asked. Then came that sly chuckle. "Whoops, let me rephrase that. Do you know anything about how to get the cockadoody cable box to work? I pushed a button on the remote and now can't get any picture. It cut off right in the middle of *Judge Judy!*"

"That's terrible," he replied, his tone grave.

He thought he heard a muffled sound from the other side of Mari's door. It might have been a low peal of laughter, and he suddenly pictured her, right there listening, not wanting to open up and get sucked into this conversation, too.

"Let me fix it for you real quick, Mrs. Faraday."

That way, hopefully the woman would keep her TV turned up really loud this evening. Meaning tomorrow, he wouldn't have to hear any comments about how she'd needed ear plugs to get to sleep the night before.

Ten minutes later, after refusing at least five offers of tea and cookies, or beer and hot dogs, he managed to get out of the woman's cluttered apartment and head for Mari's door. He lifted his hand to knock, but it swung open before he had to. She grabbed his hand and pulled him in as fast as possible, giggling as he stumbled right into her and kicked the door shut behind them.

"Hi," she said.

"Hi, yourself." He took advantage of their proximity and wrapped his arms tightly around her, bending down for a warm kiss hello. She tasted as sweet and welcoming as ever, the taste of her mouth becoming as necessary to him as his own breath.

"Miss me?" she asked when they finally ended the kiss and drew apart.

"Would I sound too sappy if I admit I've been doodling our initials on pieces of paper since yesterday?"

She snorted a laugh. "Liar."

"I've missed you," he said simply. "Are you ready to go?"

Nodding, she said, "I just need to grab something," and picked up a brightly colored gift bag from the nearby kitchen table. "Okay, ready."

He eyed the bag. "What's that?"

"It's for you."

"Crap, did I forget our anniversary?"

She chuckled. "Well, come to think of it, we did meet exactly three weeks ago today."

He made the sign of an L on his forehead. "What's the three-week anniversary gift? Paper? Silver?"

"I'm pretty sure it's rubies," she said, sounding droll.

"Okay, we'd better hit a jewelry store while we're out."

She playfully swatted his arm. "I'm kidding. It's not that kind of present. It's more of a…well…"

"What?" A thought occurred to him and his brow shot up. "Wait, is it sexy lingerie? Because if we go out to some fancy restaurant and you hand me a bag containing something sinful that you intend to wear later, you can pretty much count on us not sticking around long enough for coffee and dessert. Or, hell, a main course."

"Nope," she replied, then, her eyes twinkling, added, "Though, maybe one of these days I'll take my panties off and give them to you in a gift bag."

"I'm not entirely convinced you own any."

"Well, if you keep ripping them off me, I won't for long."

"Come on, you like the way I rip them off you."

She shivered lightly and her lids lowered a little over dreamy eyes. "Mmm. You bet I do."

He glanced at his watch, noted the time, thought about the dinner reservation… Nope. Couldn't swing it. "We'd better get out of here before I dine on you instead of fancy French food."

"I like French," she said, with a tiny, mischievous smile.

Yeah, so did he. God, just the thought of how her tongue felt in his mouth had him ready to get hard again.

"Hold that thought," he told her.

"Consider it held."

He held it, too—the thought of kissing her, tasting her, sampling every bit of her—throughout their drive downtown. Their light, flirty conversation distracted him from those images when they reached the small, romantic restaurant and were seated at a table in a private corner. But they quickly returned when he watched her sip her fruity cocktail, licking the red juice off her lips.

"Stop looking at me like that," she ordered.

"Like what?"

"Like you're Edward and I'm Bella and you want to dine on me."

He laughed softly, catching the reference. His sister, Jazz, was one of those full-grown women who'd gone *Twilight*-mad.

"I do want to dine on you, so you'd better distract me," he told her, reaching for his water and taking a deep sip.

She nodded. "I think I can do that," she said, reaching to retrieve the gift bag she'd placed under the table.

He'd forgotten all about it, to be honest. "You really shouldn't have gotten me anything."

She put the bag on the table, but kept her hand on it, not pushing it over to him. "This isn't exactly a gift—it's more like an explanation." Her throat quivered as she swallowed, as if she had to work up the nerve to say more.

Suddenly more interested, Danny leaned forward in his chair, dropping his elbows onto the table. Mari looked almost nervous, and very serious. The sexy, playful mood disappeared and he sensed that whatever she wanted to tell him—or show him—it meant a lot to her.

"Okay, I'm intrigued."

Nodding, she reached for her drink, sipped, then put it down. "Well, now that we're, uh, doing whatever it is we're doing, I feel like you should know the truth about me."

Hearing the quiver in her voice, he said, "Honey, as long as you don't tell me you're married or a transvestite, I really don't think you have anything to worry about."

She managed a faint smile. "Neither of those." Then she pushed the bag toward him. "I am, however, sort of, um…famous."

Taken completely by surprise, he ignored the bag, staring into her wide eyes. "Excuse me?"

"Well, not movie-star famous. But I, uh…well, you know I just finished getting my doctorate."

"What, did you discover the cure for cancer?"

That got a slight laugh. "Hardly. The thing is, I paid my way through school by writing."

That didn't come as too much of a shock. He'd read her article, and knew she had a gift for words.

"These are copies of my two published books."

"Seriously?" he said, his admiration for her going up even higher. "You're a published author?"

She nodded, snagged her bottom lip between her teeth, and nudged the bag closer. As he reached for the tissue at the top, more of that beautiful, kissable lip disappeared. He realized she was not just a little nervous, she was actually worried about this.

Unable to imagine why, unless she was some infamous pornographer—and, damn, with her sexual prowess, she probably could be—he reached into the bag and retrieved the two oversize paperbacks. His gaze first went to the author's name. "Mad-Mari?"

"That's me."

Huh. It fit. He hadn't seen her angry very often, but a

mad Mari was pretty formidable. At the very least, she was pretty damned sarcastic.

Then he saw the titles. And began to cough into his fist.

Mari—his sexy, romantic, irresistible Mari—had written books called *Why Do Men Suck?* and *Thanks, But I'll Just Keep My Vibrator?* Was that even possible?

"I know what you're thinking," she said.

"Oh, yeah?" he asked, wondering how she could know, when he, himself, hadn't decided yet.

"You're thinking I'm a man-bashing feminist or something."

No, he wasn't thinking that. He hadn't been thinking that at all. Quite the opposite, in fact. The first coherent thought that had crossed his mind was that somebody had really broken her heart. Which just pissed him off. "Who was he?"

"Huh?"

"The guy who hurt you enough to make you write these books?"

She shook her head slowly. "There was no guy. Well, no specific guy."

Meaning there were a bunch of them? He couldn't deny a twinge of discomfort at that thought. He was no saint, but, damn, he didn't want to think of Mari having been involved with a whole boatload of men before him.

"And no," she said, as if reading his mind, "I was not some tramp who let herself get used by a bunch of guys."

He breathed a sigh of relief, then waited for her explanation.

"The truth is, I dated a normal amount, never considered myself in love and never had my heart broken."

He gestured toward the titles. And so she told him the whole story. How she'd started a blog during college. How she'd made kvetching about bad dates a regular feature of that blog. About how it had exploded in popularity, catching the eye of an agent, who'd suggested she try writing a humorous self-help book.

And that was it. End of story. She'd done it, made a lot of women laugh, achieved some success, made some money. A bona fide success story. And he was incredibly proud of her for it.

But none of that explained why she'd been nervous about telling him. "That's fantastic," he said, meaning it. "And I can't wait to read them."

"They're meant to be funny," she reminded him, "not insulting."

He knew her well enough to know they were meant to be a *little* insulting. But hell, her wicked sense of humor was one of the things he liked best about her.

"I can take it," he told her. Then, reaching for his drink, pretending he wasn't keenly interested in hearing the rest of the story, he added, "So what haven't you told me yet?"

"Pardon?"

That was about as guilty an expression as he'd ever seen on her face. "Come on, spill it. I know there's more. We haven't gotten to the good part yet."

She closed her eyes briefly, took a deep breath, then gave him the rest of it in one long, rushed explanation. "I still have my blog. I still write as Mad-Mari every day. It's fun and it's silly and I have a lot of loyal followers. But you wouldn't be interested. You'd hate it in fact, so please, I want you to promise me that you won't visit it."

He looked at her face, flushing redder by the minute, and the truth exploded into his brain like a lightning bolt.

"Oh, shit."

She dropped her eyes.

"I'm on there, aren't I?"

"Not by name, description, rank or address," she whispered. "There's absolutely nothing that would give away your identity, Danny, I promise. Nobody who read it would ever know I was talking about you."

"Except me," he replied.

She nodded weakly.

"Uh, dare I guess when these particular blog posts went up?"

Her silence was answer enough.

Mari had obviously sounded off about her anger when she thought she'd been used and ditched. The cyber world must have gotten an earful during those two weeks after their first amazing night together. She'd probably taken the girl-bitch-session to a whole new level and undoubtedly made him the target of disdain for a whole lot of single women.

"I guess I should be glad they can't identify me," he mumbled. "I'd hate to think I have to constantly be looking over my shoulder, worried a feminist hit squad is on my tail."

"I'm so sorry."

He nodded, believing her, trying to analyze his feelings about this. On the surface of it, he was a little concerned, embarrassed. On a deeper level, he could only wonder how very upset she must have been to take her anger public.

He hated that he'd hurt her that way. And he never wanted to do it again.

Seeing her trepidation, knowing she was waiting for

him to react, he reached across the table and twined his fingers in hers. "It's okay, I'm not upset."

She made no effort to hide her relief. "Really?"

"Really." Then, realizing something, he added, "You know, you could have just deleted those entries, but you didn't."

"That's cowardly."

"True, but understandable, now that we're…" He didn't say dating, or lovers, or crazy about each other. Honestly, he didn't know how to describe what they were. So he simply said, "Together. I might never have known about them, but you came clean. I appreciate that."

"Thank you for being so understanding. I promise, I won't do it again. I've already instituted a much more close-mouthed policy on the blog."

He reached for a bread stick, offering her a sly look. "You mean you haven't gone back on there and told them you've been shagged to within an inch of your life this week?"

She gave him that look—that warm, sensual look that told him where her mind had gone. "You mean, I still have an inch left?"

He gave as good as he got. "You can have as many inches as you want."

Her eyes closed and her lips parted on a breath. She shifted a little in her chair, and he'd guarantee she'd been just as instantly hit with desire as he'd been.

"I could use a lot," she whispered. "I could use them right now, as a matter of fact. Damn, I should have worn panties tonight."

His hand tightened reflexively, and the bread stick snapped in half. "Don't," he warned her.

She didn't reply in words. Instead she shifted her leg under the table, until it brushed against his, her soft calf pressing against his firm one. Blood and heat roared through him at the thought of how beautiful those thighs were, how much he loved having them wrapped around his hips. At the idea that, once again, she was wearing absolutely nothing underneath her pretty green sundress.

"You're evil," he told her.

"Oh, no, I'm not. Give me a chance and I'll show you how nice I can be."

He glanced at the table, holding only their empty glasses and a bread basket. They hadn't even placed their dinner order yet. "What kind of date would I be if I suggested ditching this place and grabbing a pizza on the way home?"

"How about you dine on me, instead?"

That was it. The end. Any hunger for food disappeared, as did worries about whether this had been enough of a real date for her. Without a word, he rose from his chair, pulled his wallet out of his back pocket and peeled a fifty out of it, figuring that ought to cover two drinks, even in a place this swanky.

She shoved the books back in the gift bag, swooped it up and put her hand in his outstretched one. They walked quickly out of the restaurant, straight to his car, which was parked in a small lot behind the building. It was dark, crowded with vehicles, but, as far as he could see, no people.

"I can't wait. I've got to kiss you," he told her as soon as they both got in and shut the doors.

She did him one better, sliding over from the passenger seat onto his lap. Danny reached for the seat release and slid it back as far as it would go, making room for her to straddle his thighs. At the feel of that womanly warmth pressed against the seam of his pants, he jerked up, watching her mouth fall open in a pleased little cry.

Then that beautiful mouth was on his, kissing him deeply. She tasted sweet and fruity—like the drink—and their tongues swirled and tangled together as if they couldn't drink enough. Every thrust of their tongues was matched by one of their bodies as they mimicked the deep, sultry sex they both craved, and could be having, if not for a couple of layers of material.

Oh, and the possibility of an arrest for indecent exposure.

"We shouldn't..."

"Yes, we should," she insisted. Then, like Eve the temptress herself, she reached down and pulled her dress up to her waist, leaning back a little so he could see.

Panties.

"You *lied* to me?" he asked, pretending to be offended.

Her wicked smile told him she had a secret, and when she guided his hand to the seam of her silky white underwear, he realized what it was. A tiny metal tab at the top told him there was a zipper holding the undergarment together between her luscious thighs. When unzipped, it would offer complete access to all the lovely secrets between them.

"It's not even my birthday and I get to unwrap *two* presents tonight?" he whispered, unable to resist tugging that zipper down, slowly, carefully. He just wanted a tiny sample, a brief touch. He'd find that sweet little clit of hers, pleasure her, which would pleasure him, then get them out of here.

But when he moved the tab all the way down and slid his fingers into the slit, he realized he needn't have worried about catching her pretty curls with the zipper's teeth. Because there weren't many of them left, just a tiny tuft right above her pubis.

Heat and lust exploded in him when he felt the bare lips of her sex, creamy, plump and swollen. "You gotta be kidding me…"

Her eyes gleamed with wantonness as she stared down at him, licking her lips. "I hear oral sex is amazing like this."

Oh, man, did he want to find out. He'd love to drop his seat all the way back into a reclining position, sit her on his face, and feast on her for an hour. But that was crazy, risky, dangerous. It was wild enough to have her on his lap, with her dress covering most of what was going on below the waist. No way could he devour her the way he wanted to.

"Please," she whispered, riding him a little harder.

"This is nuts."

"There is nobody around," she insisted, casting another glance around the lot, dark with shadows and utterly devoid of sound.

"Just an appetizer before the drive home," he insisted, knowing he couldn't possibly resist her.

She appeared triumphant as she reached for his pants, unzipping and releasing him. He jerked into her palm, thrilled by the coolness of her skin against his hot, rock-hard dick. Then she moved over it, rubbing all that slick bareness over him, wetting him with her body's arousal.

Danny groaned, awash with sensation as skin touched skin. He was dying for her, desperate for a quick thrust. *Just one…two, max. Then we'll go.*

"I've got this covered," she told him when he reached for his pocket. "Did you know they still make diaphragms?"

"Thank God," he muttered, even more excited at the thought of being inside her with no barrier at all.

And then he was. Mari settled back onto him, the loose skirt of her dress draped almost modestly over them both, and sunk onto his cock in one slow, steady motion. He wrapped his arms around her waist, caressing the soft skin of her back, revealed by the sundress. It felt so good, so very good. Though part of him wanted to pound and writhe, he also wanted to savor the moment. So he remained still, looking up at her, noting the utter bliss on her face. Marissa Marshall was beautiful anytime, but right now, she looked absolutely ethereal.

She sighed with pleasure, then opened her eyes and looked down at him. "Mmm."

He nodded, shifting his hips a little, drawing another soft groan from deep in her throat. Lifting his hands to her hair, he rubbed its silkiness, and drew her down to him so they could kiss again. Despite their frenzy of a few minutes ago, now that they were joined, they both seemed content to go slow, easy. He kissed her gently on the lips, then moved his mouth to her jaw, her neck, to the lobe of her ear. Each gentle kiss was accompanied by a tender stroke, a soft thrust.

"Sweet," she murmured.

He understood the reaction. It was sweet, tender, something to savor rather than race through. Which was just crazy considering they were sitting in a parked car in a public parking lot.

But right now, holding her, feeling her wrapped around him, he honestly didn't care. And neither did she. They just continued to make love right there, oblivious to all the rest of the world. Until, finally, she whimpered her release, and he let go, too, filling her with every ounce of himself.

10

Wednesday 6/1/11, 07:00 a.m.
www.mad-mari.com/2011/06/01/June
Happy June!

Unlike when I said in December that it was my favorite month because of Christmas, or when I said it was March, because my birthday's in March and I always get to drink green beer, June really is my favorite month.

Summer has started to spring up, but the evenings are still a little cool, the days aren't boiling hot, and all the flowers are still in bloom. Plus...those damned stink bugs haven't shown up yet. Yippie! (Come August, you'll be hearing me rant about those rotten little buggers.)

As I mentioned yesterday, I am kinda busy this week. The temp/part-time job continues later this morning. As you know, I was off on Monday for Memorial Day... and oh, what a memorable day it was!

Hey, did I happen to tell you guys that I came clean to Mr. Perfect about this blog? I warned him about what was on here, and he promised he wouldn't peek. But, uh, just in case...hey, Mr. Perfect? You're peeking!

And if he does happen to show up, be gentle, okay?

I know you all know how to play nice.

Well, some of you.

John L. from Wyoming, you really need to find another hobby, dear. The threatening emails didn't work. The love letters you're sending me now aren't, either. And no. I will NEVER tell you where I live so we can "meet up for drinks." I'm mouthy...not stupid.

Bye y'all!

Mari

P.S. What's love feel like? (Damn, now I really hope Mr. Perfect isn't peeking!) Discuss!

Friday 6/3/11, 07:00 a.m.
www.mad-mari.com/2011/06/03/Payday!
I got my first paycheck!

It's not a fortune, but it's pretty damn good for a part-time gig.

Hey, guess what: I'm going to a fancy-schmancy party tomorrow night. Guess I'd better leave my Mad-Mari mouth at home, huh?

So, what's up for your weekend?

P.S. Bad Date Friday—I haven't forgotten! Last week's "great date" discussion was nice and sweet... and boring. So come on, bring back the bad stuff. Ready? Set? GO!

"DO I LOOK OKAY?"

Her hands out to her sides, Marissa pirouetted, showing off the flared bottom of her black dress, which wisped and fluttered around her bare legs. On the couch, her brother, Adam, who dressed better than she did any day of the week, eyed her with approval.

Adam, who lived near D.C., had come up to visit today, and could always be relied on to give good advice about clothes. He had far better taste than she did, and had been the one to pick out this dress. He'd dragged her out shopping this afternoon when he'd heard that she had a date tonight.

"Fantastic," he told her, grinning widely, his handsome face radiating his excitement for her. "You're gonna knock this guy's socks off."

Well, it sure wouldn't be the first time she'd knocked Danny out of his clothes. Boy, howdy, had she ever. More times than she could remember now…and she was nowhere close to being tired of it. She honestly didn't think she'd ever grow tired of being intimate with the man.

Probably because it *was* intimate. It wasn't just body-rocking, earth-shaking sex—though, heaven knew, they'd definitely had that. But there was also such sweetness, emotion. Sometimes Danny didn't seem to want to leave her body, even after he came. He'd caress her gently, kiss her hair, stroke her cheek, whisper sweet words until they would fall asleep, still joined. And invariably, she would wake up to find him thick and hard, bringing her to insane heights of pleasure all over again.

To think—two short weeks ago, Marissa had been sure she'd never see Danny again. She'd thought she'd had the best sex of her life with somebody whose last name she would never even know; that it was all behind her. And now, here she was, thoroughly satisfied, deliciously sore from all their love-making, putting on her pretty new dress, getting ready to go with him to a semi-formal dance.

"I still can't believe you're dating a sailor."

"Naval Aviator."

"Whatever," Adam said with a wave of his hand. "You, who swore you'd never give the time of day to any guys in uniform. Going to a dance on a base…without having been tied up, gagged and dragged there."

"I know," she muttered. "It's crazy."

A part of her—the part that longed to be held in Danny's strong arms while they swayed together to some soft, sultry music—was actually looking forward to it. But a bigger part—the part that remembered that whole military lifestyle her family had lived—wanted to run like hell.

She tried not to tense up when thinking about it. Tried not to recall the screaming fights her parents would have after coming home late from some social event, where her sobbing mother would accuse her father of having disappeared with some junior officer's wife for a half hour. Then her father would counter that she was, as usual, being melodramatic and ridiculous. And Mari would open her door to her sister and brothers, who would, one by one, creep into her room and crawl into her bed. Huddled under the covers, the four of them would try desperately not to hear, occasionally able to drown out the actual words but never the angry, hurt voices.

Mari was firmly against infidelity, but sometimes she could understand why her mother had chosen to get even by going down the what's-good-for-the-goose-is-good-for-the-gander road. The woman had been driven to it by a lifetime of hurt and humiliation. But walking out not just on her faithless husband, but her own kids? Not looking back, not once, not ever?

No. That she couldn't see at all. How awful must the woman's life have been to drive her to it?

"You sure you're okay?" Adam asked, as always intuitive to her feelings. Usually cheerful and happy-go-lucky, confident about his sexuality and not one bit ashamed of his lifestyle, he was the most perceptive person she knew.

"I guess," she muttered, unable to stop a tiny wince as she let the dark thoughts creep into her mind.

"Don't," he ordered, his smile fading, and a stern-but-tender note appearing in his voice.

"Don't what?"

Rolling his eyes, he got up from the couch and came over to straighten the seam running down her back. "Don't compare this to *them*."

She didn't have to ask who he meant.

"You're nothing like *her*, and no way would you go out with anybody like *him*."

She knew he was right, logically. *Logically*.

Emotionally was another story. She didn't even know her mother anymore, so she couldn't be sure whether she was like her or not. Marissa hadn't had a real, genuine conversation with the woman in fifteen years, ever since her mom had hooked up with a diplomat while the family had been stationed in Germany, and left to be with him. An occasional phone call or, nowadays, an email, wasn't exactly a prime opportunity to get to know somebody.

Or to ask them why they abandoned you to an emotionless father in a foreign country.

She wasn't close to her father, and she never would be. Still, damn it, she gave him props for sticking around. He'd been stern and cold, but he'd been there, every day, providing them with food and shelter, trying to show up for school events when his schedule allowed. He'd been a shit as a husband, but he'd always been the best father he knew how to be—which wasn't great. But at least he'd tried.

The whole situation still gave her a headache when she thought about it.

"Stop," Adam said, swatting her on the butt. "I mean it!"

"Sorry. I guess I'm getting cold feet. Going to one of these events, where the men stick their chests out to emphasize their medals, and the wives drink too much and share all the latest gossip in their small, incestuous society, doesn't really appeal."

Danny, however, appealed to her tremendously.

"This guy must be really special to make it worthwhile."

"He is," she admitted.

Adam turned to go back to the couch, bending down to resume a game of fetch with Brionne, then innocently murmured, "So I guess you really have forgiven him for not calling for those two weeks."

Mari groaned. "You told me you never visit my blog."

A shrug lifting his shoulders, he replied, "I lied. I love it—it's my first stop every day. Believe me, I did not like watching your sad-sack meltdown after this guy bailed on you."

Sad-sack. Yes. She had been. How utterly embarrassing. God, did she ever hope Danny had kept his promise not to go there and scour through the archives.

Quickly telling her brother the whole story, including the fact that Danny had shown up here with receipts and email printouts, she saw his suspicion ease. He might play it cool most of the time, but, at heart, he was as protective of her as she was of him.

"Okay, I guess you were right to give the guy a second chance."

Before she could reply, a knock sounded on the door. "He's here," she said, butterflies leaping in her stomach. This was the first time she'd introduced Danny to anyone in her life. And of all those she loved, Adam's was the opinion that mattered the most to her. Being the closest to her in age, he'd shared some of the burden for the little ones, and the two of them had formed a bond that nothing could shake.

"Shall I answer it and be all protective big brother?"

She snickered. "You're three years younger and an inch shorter than me."

"Half an inch," he retorted, grinning as he walked to the door and opened it.

To his credit, Danny didn't reveal an ounce of surprise or suspicion that a strange man had answered the door. He merely offered Adam a friendly smile.

"You must be Danny," her brother said, not moving out of the way as he thoroughly sized the other man up.

"I guess you know me…but I can't say the same. I'm afraid I don't know you from Adam."

"I'm Mari's brother. Adam."

Danny barked a surprised laugh, which Adam echoed. Then the two men shook hands and Adam ushered him in. They immediately launched into conversation. Danny was his charming, amiable self, and she saw Adam's worry fade, his stiff posture easing as he saw what Mari had seen in Danny from day one: that he was a truly nice guy.

As usual, seeing Danny in his uniform gave Mari the

shivers—both of utter appreciation, because of how incredibly handsome he looked in it. But also of worry.

In the days when they'd been enjoying each other in every way, she'd often managed to forget who he was and what he did. When he was naked—gorgeously, deliciously naked—there was no way to tell he was a pilot who traveled the world and probably had women throwing themselves at him in every port of call.

He doesn't catch them, she reminded herself. *He's not like Dad.*

She knew that, logically, in her Dr. Marshall brain. But her Mad-Mari personality was still so unsure, so worried about trusting someone only to be hurt, she couldn't allow herself to completely accept it.

Her part-time job was almost at an end. She had only two more lectures scheduled on campus. The ones so far had been delightful—fun and engaging, with the students responding incredibly well to the Danny-and-the-Doctor show. But after the job was done, when they didn't have to work together, and wouldn't ever risk running into one another again, what would happen?

She suspected he'd want to continue seeing her. And she knew she wanted to continue seeing him.

But for how long? How long until he got called up to fly into danger, to risk his life? If they continued this affair, if she fell more deeply in love, what would happen when his shore rotation was up? He could be stationed on the other side of the world. Maybe he'd ask her to go with him? And maybe she'd even consider it, she was that crazy about him.

Then what? The lifestyle would suffocate her, the memories would overwhelm her, the doubts would fill her mind and her heart. And the resentment would grow.

So what should she do? Stick around and take what

she could get? Or just let this go when classes ended, a memory of the most wonderful spring of her life.

Finally spying her, Danny let out a low whistle of appreciation. "Wow."

Shoving away all the doubts—at least for now—she gave another little twirl. "You like it? Adam picked it out."

"I wasn't whistling at the dress," he admitted, his voice a little throaty. He didn't take his eyes off her, devouring her with an appreciative stare. As if he hadn't spent every night of the past week—until last night—in her bed. She had to wonder what it might be like being looked at like that every day for the rest of her life.

Was such a thing even possible? Probably not. Every relationship waxed and waned, the electric highs gradually mellowing to a more quiet, genuine appreciation. But something told her Danny would offer a woman he truly loved that same wolfish, appreciative, sexy look when he was eighty years old.

She wanted to be the one he offered it to.

The thought flashed through her mind, shocking her a little...but not a lot. Because, deep down, she'd already figured out she was falling in love with the man. She'd been infatuated with him at first. Now, having slept in his arms, laughed with him, shared his French fries, beaten him at poker, watched him shave, whispered about the past, she knew it was more than want. More than like. A lot more.

"Maybe we shouldn't go," Danny said, frowning. "I don't know if I can trust Quag, or anybody else, around you."

Having met his buddy, she understood the sentiment. The guy was a big-time flirt. "You can, however, trust me," she said pertly.

Adam jumped in. "You can definitely trust Mari. She's a keeper."

She rolled her eyes, then made a face at her brother, who was so obviously pushing. He must have formed a great impression of Danny to be working this hard at playing matchmaker.

"Okay, kiddies, you'd better get on your way. Danny, great meeting you." Adam reached up and straightened a curl hanging by Mari's cheek. "You look gorgeous, Cinderella. Have fun at the ball."

She did feel a little like that fairy-tale princess. She was not used to dressing up to socialize. Her most recent social engagements, while she was in school, had usually involved somber black suits, stale coffee and boring speeches.

Tonight, though, felt romantic. As if, with Danny by her side, looking at her with that tender, admiring expression, anything was possible.

Absolutely anything.

NEITHER OF THEM SAID much during the drive down to Annapolis, comfortable in the silence that had fallen between them. It wasn't that Danny didn't have something to talk about—oh, God, did he ever! In fact, he'd intended to share his incredible news with her back at her apartment, but her brother's presence had made him wait.

He didn't dare bring the subject up in the car. He was still so keyed up about it himself, he worried if he started talking about it, he'd be too distracted to drive.

Because today, the letter he'd been waiting for had arrived.

The plain white envelope with the NASA logo had almost taunted him with its thinness. As he'd reached in to retrieve it, he'd felt a little like a high schooler certain the small envelope meant he hadn't gotten into the college of his choice.

In Danny's case, though, small had worked out just fine.

He was in. He'd been accepted as an astronaut candidate. Out of the tens of thousands who'd applied for the next training rotation, he had become one of the hundred to be chosen.

He was going to be an astronaut. And if fate was kind and if he worked his ass off, then hopefully before the end of this very decade, Danny would get a first-class ticket into space.

All the years of work, the dreaming, the planning, the busting his ass to get the best grades, the best performance scores, the best ratings, the best missions—had paid off. The dream that had seized him as a little boy was finally coming true.

He didn't know who had cried harder when he called home to tell his family—his mom, out of excitement and worry. Or his dad, out of sheer, unadulterated pride.

Finally landing his dream job was the cake and the icing. But the cherry on top, making the day even better, was that sitting right beside him was the kind of woman he'd always dreamed of having, too.

A beautiful, funny, smart-as-hell, sexy, lovable woman who he was crazy about.

He knew he wasn't totally in the clear yet. Mari would almost certainly be glad to hear he'd be leaving the navy much sooner than she'd expected. Plus, Houston would probably sound a lot more appealing to her than some tiny base in a foreign country. Until he got her to admit that they did have a future together, however, he wasn't counting his unhatched chickens.

When they reached Annapolis, Danny parked at the yacht club where tonight's gala was being held. But rather than leading Mari into the brightly lit building, from which the sounds of music and laughter could easily be heard, he took her arm and steered her toward the docks.

"Can we walk for a minute? I need to talk to you."

She stiffened for just a second, as if expecting bad news.

"Something wonderful has happened," he told her. "Something I've wanted for a long time."

Appearing curious, she relaxed, nodded and said, "I can't wait to hear more."

When they reached the shoreline, they turned to walk along the pier, the path easily lit by the bright moon-and-starlit sky above. The water lapped gently against the sides of the beautiful boats moored here, and sea birds continue to swoop in the darkness, calling out their melodic cries. The air was thick with brine—clean and cool, sharp to the mouth. He licked his lips and tasted salt there, knowing if he kissed Mari now, her mouth would taste just as spicy.

"So what's going on?" she asked, breaking the silence.

He stopped, and looked up at the sky. "Beautiful, isn't it?" Unable to take his eyes off the moon, its mysterious glow somehow brighter tonight than it had ever been before, he continued. "I think I've told you that ever since I was a kid, and my dad took me out to watch the planes landing at O'Hare, all I ever wanted to do was fly."

"You sort of told me," she murmured. Then, with a soft laugh, she added, "I misunderstood the first time—I thought you meant you wanted to be a mechanic."

Remembering their first day, he joined in her laughter. Though it had only been a month's time, they'd come a long way from the guy who'd been fascinated by the girl who'd hidden her panties in the glove box.

"Well, what I haven't told you is that it isn't just air flight I want." He raised his arm, pointing toward the moon, closing one eye so that his own finger seemed to block out the enormous globe. "I want *that*."

"The moon?" she asked, sounding amused.

"Eventually."

Oh, how he hoped man would return there in his lifetime.

"I think there's a star registry, so I might be able to swing one of those, but the moon's a little tougher to get."

He turned to face her. "I want to *go* there, Mari."

Her amusement faded, and her eyes widened with wonder. She was a smart woman and immediately grasped what he meant.

"You want to be an astronaut?"

He corrected her. "I'm *going* to be an astronaut."

She gaped.

"I found out today. I've been accepted into the Astronaut Candidate Training Program. I leave for Houston in four weeks."

"Oh, my God," she whispered, sounding stunned.

He wasn't sure how she'd react—if she'd be afraid, be upset that he hadn't told her, complain that he was leaving.

None of those. Instead, she graced him with a warm, genuine smile, her eyes glittering in the moonlight. She looked as pleased for him as he felt for himself. "Congratulations, Danny, that's *incredible* news."

Relieved, excited, jubilant, he pulled her into his arms

and kissed her deeply, loving the taste of genuine happiness on her lips. She never ceased to surpass every one of his expectations. He had expected she'd be glad for him. But she seemed beyond thrilled.

When the kiss ended, he kept his arms around her waist. Hers were looped around his neck, and she stared up at him intently, as if memorizing his face, trying to get to know him all over again.

"You're really going into space?" she whispered.

"If fate continues to be kind. I've got a lot of training—years—to get through. But someday…God willing, someday."

She moved a hand to his face, tenderly cupping his cheek, rubbing her thumb across his bottom lip. "You will be wonderful," she said, sounding completely sure about it.

"You know what this means," he said, wondering if it was too soon to ask her how she'd like living in Houston. Not right away—the first year of training would be harrowing. Not that he could wait a year—no way could he be without her for that long. But maybe he could go ahead and she could take a couple of months to pack up, look for a job and move.

It sounded like a good idea to him, anyway. He only hoped she'd feel the same way.

But before he could even broach the subject, a voice interrupted them. "There you are—there's my main man. Come on, dude, the whole party's waiting to congratulate you!"

Shocked by Quag's intrusion, he released Mari and the two of them turned to watch his friend jog over.

"Midas, seriously, way to go. The news just broke." He threw his arms around Danny's shoulders, giving him a rib-crushing hug. "Congratulations, I knew you could do it! You are on your way to the stars."

Stunned, since he had told nobody other than his parents, and now Mari, about his letter, he could only mumble, "What…how…"

"The Commandant got a call from somebody in Houston. This is big news, buddy-boy." He turned to Mari and winked. "You ready to be a space-superstar's number one fangirl?"

Beside him Mari stiffened the tiniest bit. Danny hid a groan, appreciative that his friend was so happy for him, but not liking the timing. He really would have liked a few more minutes with Mari, to gauge how she felt about this.

Oh, he knew she was happy for him. What he wanted to know was how she saw it affecting their relationship. And that fangirl crack wasn't helping.

Danny tightened his arm across her shoulders. "She's a whole hell of a lot more than that," he told his friend.

In fact, he hoped she would one day be a space-super…er, an *astronaut's* wife.

Because he loved her. Real, lifelong, can't-live-without-you love. Fate or serendipity be damned. They might have brought her to him, but every day and night he'd spent in her company had reinforced his feelings for this woman.

She was his fate. She was his serendipity.

She was everything he wanted.

Mari…and space.

"Let's go, let's go, the Commandant ordered champagne for the entire party!"

Offering Mari an apologetic look, he let Quag push him toward the club. He kept his fingers laced with Mari's. He wanted her by his side throughout the evening, knowing her fast mind was working double-time. Those negative ideas she always managed to come up with had to be whispering in her ear.

But once they got inside, he was surrounded by well-wishers—superiors, navy brass, colleagues at the school, other pilots—and he and Mari were separated. He kept his gaze moving over the crowd, trying to keep tabs on her location despite the constant conversations and handshakes. He'd always find her—she was the most beautiful woman in the room. Sometimes she'd be chatting with Quag, or with a few other faculty members she'd gotten to know. Each time, she'd catch his eye, offer him a thumbs-up that said she didn't mind being on her own, and Danny would be dragged away for another congratulatory conversation.

It was at least an hour before he was finally able to stop talking and get a minute alone. He spent that minute scouring the reception hall, then the rest of the club, looking for Mari. He wanted to apologize, wanted to pull her into the nearest closet and kiss any doubts out of her mind. Hell, even a simple dance would be nice.

"I think she went to the ladies' room," a voice said.

Seeing a fellow teacher, a woman who the boys called the Admiral because she was so tough on her students, he said, "Excuse me?"

"Doctor Marshall. You came with her tonight, didn't you?"

He nodded.

"I passed her on her way to the powder room."

"Okay, thanks."

"Oh, and Commander Wilkes?"

"Yes?"

"It's nice to see you two finally decided to take your romance out of the classroom and into the real world."

He blanched for a second, remembering the more graphic romantic moments he and Mari had shared in the classroom.

"The rumors about your lectures have gotten around campus."

Seeing the twinkle of humor in her eye, and knowing she was referring to student gossip, he breathed a sigh of relief and offered her a good-natured nod. "Thanks for the help."

As the teacher walked away, he realized she was right—it was well past time to bring their romance out into the light, make it official. He only hoped Mari wouldn't run like hell when he suggested it.

Following the signs, he headed down a side corridor of the building, where the opulent restrooms were located. He intended to plant himself outside the door and make sure she didn't get past him. But before that door swung open, a side one—a smaller, second entrance that led directly to the valet parking area—did.

Danny glanced over, seeing a petite, dark-haired woman enter.

Then he froze. Because it had suddenly hit him—the identity of that petite woman.

"Oh, my God," he said, doing a double take.

"Danny!" she squealed.

Striding toward her, he caught his little sister in his arms and swung her around, shocked, stunned, but so damned happy to see her he couldn't speak. Like she had when they were kids, Jazz wrapped around him like a spider monkey, her arms around his shoulders, her legs around his waist, squeezing him like she hadn't seen him in five years, rather than the five months since he'd gone home for the holidays.

"Am I interrupting?" a cool voice asked.

Laughter on his lips, Danny turned around, still holding his crazy, feisty little sister, and saw Mari standing right outside the bathroom. She'd obviously come out and seen them.

And she didn't look very happy.

"Oh, hell, this looks bad," he mumbled, realizing what she must think.

"Only if she's your girlfriend," his sister said, her pert voice sounding amused. "Is she your girlfriend?"

He slowly lowered Jazz to the floor.

"No, I'm not his girlfriend," Mari insisted, her chin lifted in that familiar snooty-teacher pose that he hadn't seen in a couple of weeks. "So, feel free to continue whatever you were…doing."

Danny had never figured Mari to be the jealous type, but right now, she looked ready to fry Jazz with a glare. He certainly didn't like putting her in that position—but had to admit, it was kind of cute. It was also nice to know she felt a little territorial about him. That sort of hinted that she thought they were in a relationship. *Progress.*

"Mari, I'd like you to meet Jazz." Noogeying his sibling on the head, he added, "My obnoxious kid sister."

Mari's mouth dropped open on an audible gasp, then a flush slowly crept into her cheeks. "Oh, my God. You're Jazzie girl?"

"Yep, that's me!" Without waiting for a response, Jazz strode over and stuck her hand out.

Mari took it, saying, "I'm so sorry. I shouldn't have assumed…"

"Don't sweat it, you were every inch a lady. If I'd have walked out and seen some ho-bag wrapped around my man, I'da come out swinging."

"Gee, stop to talk to a valet and you get accused of picking up a ho-bag," a man's voice said.

Glancing back, Danny saw Blake Marshall, his sister's fiancé, approaching, apparently having followed Jazz through the side door.

Jazz winked as she sauntered over to the man who'd finally tamed the wild-child of the Wilkes clan. "Hey, at least you've been properly warned."

"Or the ho-bags have."

"Seen any?"

"Nary a one," he replied. Then the two of them laughed, so visibly in love, they were a testament to possibility. Because nobody had ever seen tough, ballsy Jazz ending up with a man as conservative, upstanding and *nice* as Blake. Yet they now seemed absolutely perfect for one another.

"It's great to see you, Blake," Danny said, reaching out to shake his future brother-in-law's hand.

"I can't believe I ruined your family reunion by being such a judgmental bitch," Mari said, shaking her head. "Please, forgive me."

Danny went to her side, put an arm across her shoulder and tugged her over for a proper introduction. Still looking embarrassed as hell, she mumbled, "I'm really sorry, Danny. Feel free to meow at me for real this time—I deserve it."

"Forget it," he told her.

"You were so nice when Adam opened the door."

"Adam? Who's Adam?" asked Jazz. "An ex?"

"Her brother," Danny explained.

"Well, don't feel too bad. I bet your brother didn't have his arms and legs wrapped around you when Danny showed up," Jazz said.

The ice finally breaking, Mari laughed. The tension

in her body eased. Her jaw loosened, and her smile widened, and she warmly greeted Jazz and Blake.

Danny felt his own moment of tension ease, too. "I still cannot believe you two are here."

"Are you kidding?" Blake replied. "As soon as your mom told us your big news, Jazz called and badgered Amanda into flying us out here."

Amanda was his kid sister's best friend, and boss at a small regional carrier located at O'Hare. Blake worked in customer relations at the airport, and Jazz was a top airline mechanic. Between the two of them, they had some pretty great contacts when it came to quick travel.

Jazz explained, "Your friend Quag told us you'd be here tonight and arranged to get us on the guest list to surprise you."

"Believe me, I'm surprised."

Maybe even as surprised as Mari had looked when she'd walked out of the bathroom and seen him in the embrace of another woman.

He kept thinking of that expression as the four of them returned to the dance, laughing and chatting the night away. Because, while she seemed fine, and was obviously embarrassed by her assumption, a shadow seemed to have come across Mari's mood. Though she and Jazz got along like they'd known each other forever—Mari had found another woman who could match her occasional snarkiness—her laughter wasn't quite as bright. And every once in a while he caught her looking at him with a tender, yet almost sad expression.

But he didn't know why. He couldn't understand the sadness.

At least, not until very late that night when he took her home and walked with her into her apartment.

Because, to his extreme shock, when he reached out

to draw her into his arms, Mari turned her tear-stained face to him and said, "I'm so happy for you Danny. I really am. But I think it's best if we just end this now."

11

MARI HADN'T MEANT TO blurt it out like that. If Adam had asked her this afternoon whether this would be her last evening with Danny, not only would she would denied it, she would have been horrified by the idea.

Now, though, it appeared to be true.

They had to end this. She'd been worrying about where the affair was heading, and now she knew: toward heartache and pain.

Time to cut her losses. Let him go while she still could, before she lost every ounce of herself in him and could never find her way away out again.

"What did you say?"

"It's over, Danny. I'm sorry, I don't want to see you anymore."

She certainly hadn't meant to say it so abruptly, tonight of all nights, when Danny's dreams were taking off and he was so happy. But she'd done it anyway, her vocal cords driven by an irrational panic that had gripped her when he'd reached for her.

The roiling emotions she'd been feeling all evening had made her stomach churn and her heart turn to stone. It wasn't just what she'd felt when she'd walked out and seen him hugging a strange woman—she'd been sure she would throw up. It went back even earlier, when she'd spent the evening watching the way Danny's entire world had changed.

For the better, she knew that. His life was about to become a kind of fairy-tale adventure. She was genuinely thrilled for him about it.

But it wasn't *her* adventure. She knew it, even if, deep down, he hadn't realized that yet. Tonight, every time she turned around and saw some woman making a play for him—and there had been a lot—or heard another person call him an astrostud, or a groupie-luring space-star, she'd become a little more certain that she couldn't stick around to watch it happen.

"You can't be serious," he finally said after a long, stunned silence.

"I'm sorry, but I am."

She turned away from him, walking into her small kitchen, needing a glass of cold water to keep her head clear and her emotions firmly in check. Mostly to keep him from pulling her into his arms as he'd been about to do.

That would have been disastrous. Because she had known he would kiss her. And his wonderful kisses would lead to her bedroom. And in the morning, maybe she would have allowed their incredible lovemaking to dull her senses, make her forget some of what she'd felt tonight.

"Explain this to me," he ordered, following her into the kitchen.

She sipped her water. "We knew it was going to end soon. And now, well, you're leaving for Houston in a month…"

"You think that when I leave for Houston, that'll be it?"

"I honestly have been wondering if we'd even see each other after this week," she admitted.

He reached for her, but she ducked away.

"Mari, I'm crazy about you. And you're crazy about me."

"That's besides the point."

He ran a frustrated hand through his golden-brown hair, looking weary and confused. He'd gone from a very high high earlier tonight, to feeling kicked in the teeth by her, and she felt like pure shit about it. Mari's heart ached. She wanted to reach out and touch him, tell him she didn't mean it—tell him she was falling in love with him.

But she didn't. Doing so would make their inevitable breakup even more painful.

Knowing she owed him more of an explanation, she took a deep breath, released it and said, "Danny, I told you how I feel about your lifestyle. I don't want to move all over the world, don't want to interact with all the same fish in the same small military pond. I don't want to worry every day about losing somebody I care about."

He frowned. "But I won't be flying into combat anymore."

"No, you'll be flying off the damn planet!" she said, thinking of the recent tragedies in the American space program.

"Not for a long time, and probably not more than a handful of times in my entire life."

Her instinctive worry for him wasn't the biggest issue. "There's still the whole military world. I grew up in it, and I am never going back."

"My assignment to NASA means I won't be living the navy life."

"I know, but in some ways, the space one will be worse."

His jaw dropped. "What?"

"Look, this country loves its heroes. And astronauts are at the top of the list. You'll be wined and dined, you'll have to schmooze and attend all the right events with the right people."

"Are you kidding? For the first couple of years I'll be attending mind-numbing classes and wondering what the hell I've gotten myself into!"

She patiently continued making her point. "But eventually, you're going to become *that* guy. That sexy, charming hero who, when he's not off saving the world from a rogue asteroid is traveling across the globe, meeting dignitaries, attending balls, speaking at conferences, patting the heads of schoolchildren." She swallowed hard, then added, "The guy every woman makes a play for."

"Oh," he said, his eyes widening. He slowly shook his head. "This is about me hugging my sister?"

"No!" she insisted. "It's about how I felt about being such a jealous bitch when you hugged your sister."

"For God's sake, Mari, I'm not some horny kid. I am thirty-three years old, I finished sowing my oats years ago…before I nearly bought it in an Afghan desert and realized there's a whole lot more to life than nailing the women who want to notch their bedpost with a fighter pilot."

She winced, surprised by his bluntness, though not by his words. He'd told her about what had happened to him early in the war, when he'd been shot down outside of Kandahar. Those hours he'd spent alone, waiting to die, hoping to live, not knowing what his life would be like when he got back, just knowing he wanted to get there. His words had touched her heart, and she'd spent a long time that night, gently kissing the scar on his leg, thankful he'd been spared.

"I know you're not some kind of ladies' man, Danny. It's not that I think you'd cheat…"

"I wouldn't."

"I know that, I trust you.…" God, how to explain this. "But I also know myself. I know you're going to be *that* bright, golden guy. I am just terrified that I'm then going to turn into *that* woman. I'm smart and I'm educated and I've got a hell of a career ahead of me. I don't want to be the insecure girlfriend, the one who gets jealous and starts wondering where you are and who you're with. Not ever."

He crossed his arms and leaned across the doorjamb. "Why don't you admit the truth? You're scared you're too much like your *mother.*"

She said nothing, unable to deny it. She'd talked to him about her childhood. She'd spent a lifetime resenting her abandonment by her mother, knowing it had been driven by the older woman's unhappiness over the way she was living. So how could she voluntarily sign up for that same kind of life?

No, Danny wasn't a cheat like her father—she truly believed that. But who was to say she wouldn't be jealous and insecure, anyway, driving him to it…like her dad used to accuse her mother of doing?

"You're headed for a rock star's life," she whispered.

"Oh, sure, astronauts are always stalked by groupies."

"No," she snapped. "They're stalked by desperate

women who put on diapers and drive across the country in one night, threatening to kill their romantic competition."

He gaped, but didn't ask what she was talking about. Everyone in the country had heard that sordid story a few years ago about an astronaut affair gone wrong, and a woman who'd taken desperate measures to hold on to her man.

"Jesus, you really have this all figured out, huh?" For the first time, Danny wasn't eyeing her with gentleness or regret. Instead, as his shoulders straightened and his jaw grew stiff and hard, he cast her a look that was beyond disappointed.

"Thanks for thinking so highly of me."

"Danny…"

"Save it. You know, Mari, I feel sorry for you. You've spent most of your life in hiding. You're desperately trying to make sure nobody ever gets the chance to hurt you the way you were hurt as a kid. You buried yourself in school, you hide behind a website, share your feelings with the entire world online and in print, but only because you're too scared to ever admit them in person."

She flinched. He turned to leave.

"Danny, it's not that I don't care about…"

"Don't say it," he snapped, his stride not slowing. "Don't say another word. I don't want to hear any more."

Mari watched, her heart in her throat. She was getting what she'd wanted, right? So why was a scream welling up in her throat? Why did her hands tremble as she lifted them, as if her very fingers could claw the words she'd just said out of the air and make this entire devastating ten-minute conversation disappear?

He reached the door and opened it. But before stepping out, he turned to her and gave her a pitying look. "I always thought you were just self-protective and pessimistic because of some past hurts. But the truth is, Mari, you're a damned coward."

She opened her mouth to reply, even though she didn't know what she should say.

I'm sorry. Stop. I didn't mean it.

I love you.

All of the above?

But before she could say anything, Danny was striding down the hall, toward the stairs. Never looking back, he turned the corner and disappeared until just the echo of his footsteps remained. And then that echo, like the man she loved, was gone.

She remained very still, absorbing it all. Tears filled her eyes as she wondered what in the name of heaven she'd just done.

"He's wrong about one thing," a voice said.

Shocked, she swung around to see Mrs. Faraday, eyeing her from behind her slightly open door.

"What?"

"You're not just a coward, hon," the woman said with a disgusted grunt. "You're a freaking idiot."

Sunday, 6/2/11, 03:38 a.m.
www.mad-mari.com/2011/06/02/ohgod
    Tonight I made the biggest mistake of my life.
    I am, indeed, a coward.
    Only I don't know how to make it right.

IT TOOK DANNY A GOOD thirty-six hours to calm down after his last conversation with Mari—the woman he loved, and truly believed he could love for the rest of his life.

The woman who'd dumped him for fear of what he could, might, *maybe* would do in some possible future scenario. He had tried to wrap his mind around that long after he'd left her Saturday night, and it still made absolutely zero sense to him.

Having houseguests—Jazz and Blake—he'd had to hide his anger throughout the next day, not wanting to relive the conversation with his sister. She had, of course, realized something was wrong. But, for a change—probably under Blake's influence—Jazz hadn't harassed him into revealing what it was. She'd merely put a soft hand on his shoulder, whispering, "It'll be okay," before leaving for the airport that evening.

Once alone again, he'd spent the night in his apartment, listening to voice mail after voice mail from old friends and new ones, colleagues and family members, all of whom wanted to congratulate him. He couldn't deny it, though he was still incredibly happy about his professional future, the screwup with his personal one had definitely put a damper on things. He'd barely gotten two hours of sleep, torn between thinking about going out and getting drunk, or driving up to Baltimore and making Mari admit she was in love with him.

"She is," he told himself Monday morning.

He knew she loved him. She didn't have to say the words.

The problem wasn't lack of love. It was lack of trust, lack of confidence, lack of courage.

And those things Lieutenant Commander Danny Wilkes simply could not do without.

So he stayed home. Right through the starting time of their class, when he knew Mari would be heading to give one of her last two lectures to the students.

"She'll do just fine without you," he told himself.

Just fine.

Knowing he needed to stay busy, if only so he wouldn't give in to the impulse to go over there and accidentally-on-purpose bump into her, he opened his laptop and began doing a little research on life in Houston. But when he went to type in the letters for his favorite search engine, he found himself typing in something else.

Mad-Mari.com

He'd promised not to visit the site, and he hadn't. He'd read one of her books—enjoying the hell out of it, even though some of her rants might have been a little scary to a lesser man. But he'd not searched for her online world.

"Hell, we're not together anymore," he muttered. So the promise didn't count.

The screen was slow to load, but finally came up. He saw the cute cartoon graphic of a character who looked like Mari—beautiful ash-blond hair, huge eyes, big smile. Then he saw her most recent post.

It had gone up before dawn Sunday morning, hinting Mari had had as sleepless a night as his own.

Zeroing in on the message, which was stark and painfully brief in the middle of the large, empty screen, he read the words, thought about them, then read them again.

The biggest mistake of my life.

His heart began to beat a little faster. His fingers tingled on the keyboard, and his breath got caught in his throat.

I was a coward, and I don't know how to make it right.

If she meant it—if she truly regretted it, knew she'd been driven merely by fear, and wanted to fix things—she should have come to him. Shown up at his door.

And maybe she would, this morning, after her class. Or maybe she'd thought she'd see him here and ask him if they could talk.

Or, damn it, maybe he would just go find her and ask for an explanation.

Oh. And get her back.

MARI TRIED HARD TO MAINTAIN her enthusiasm when delivering her lecture, but, once she'd realized that Danny definitely wasn't going to be there, it proved difficult. The midshipmen were almost as disappointed as she was. Word of his appointment to NASA had spread and they all wanted to congratulate him and hear details of what he'd done to get where he was.

Part of her had suspected he wouldn't come. Why would he? She'd been horrible to him Saturday night, raining on one of the biggest nights of his entire life like a spoiled ten-year-old.

God, she regretted it. So much.

Maybe if she hadn't been talking to Adam earlier that day, she would have handled things better. If only she hadn't been remembering those awful nights, recalling all the fights, her father's affairs, her mother's tears. If only those things hadn't flashed in her mind every time someone reminded the room of Danny's brilliant future—the fame, the women. Or when she'd spied him embracing his own kid sister.

If only she hadn't allowed herself to remember what it was like to be abandoned.

Danny wouldn't abandon you.

He wouldn't betray her.

He was too decent, too noble and too honest a man. He wore his emotions on his handsome face, goodness radiating from every inch of him. From the warmth of his smile, to the tenderness of his voice, to the thought-fulness he displayed toward everyone around him, he was, undoubtedly, the best man she'd ever known.

An ultimate officer and a gentleman. A man who deserved her utter trust…a man she knew, deep down, she *did* trust.

And she'd thrown him away.

"You're so damned stupid," she muttered.

"Huh?" asked a student sitting in the front row. He straightened in his seat. Actually, all the young men, who'd almost appeared to be dozing during what she, herself, acknowledged was a pretty boring speech, eyed her with sudden interest.

She stared around the room, crowded wall-to-wall with youngsters sitting in every available chair and space, evaluating her words.

"I said I was stupid," she finally admitted.

"Why? What'd you do?"

"Something that you guys probably never do—I played it safe."

"Hey, I play it safe," one voice called, his tone a little suggestive. "I buy condoms by the case!"

"Why, so you can use 'em for water balloons?" another said, drawing laughter from the room.

Her tense shoulders eased a bit. She liked these young men. Liked interacting with them. Actually, she liked it so much, she was giving serious thought to doing something with her doctoral degree that she hadn't even considered before.

Going back to school.

Not as a student this time, but as a teacher. A psychology professor.

She suspected she might be very good at teaching young coeds just starting out on their college careers.

Not with life lessons, like the ones she'd talked about here, but with actual courses. The idea had interested her enough that she'd put in a call to her old favorite professor up at Hopkins, asking whether the university was looking for fresh academic blood in the Psychology Department.

Of course, that was before Saturday night. Before she'd realized Danny would be moving to Houston.

Before she'd decided she wanted to go with him.

He won't want you to.

Maybe not. But she wasn't willing to let him go without taking one last chance to fix this. She need to apologize, needed to admit that she loved him…and trusted him. And she needed to do it to his face.

Which she would. Once class was over, she'd march over to his apartment and knock until he answered. There was no nosy next-door neighbor to tell her if he was there, but there was the possibility that his fiery sister would answer. If so, she might slam the door shut again—or worse. But Marissa was willing to take that chance.

He was worth it. *They* were worth it.

"Actually," she said once the room had quieted, "I was talking about playing it emotionally safe. I was a coward, following my head instead of my emotions. And now I regret it." *Bitterly.*

"Love stuff, huh?"

She managed a smile. "Yeah, I know, at eighteen that's probably the last thing you're interested in. But someday, you might not mind so much."

"Did some dude break your heart?"

Actually, no. She'd done that all on her own, breaking both her heart, and, possibly, Danny's.

"'Cause if he did, we'll kick his ass," another said. "You're one of us now."

She began to smile, ready to thank the young man, when another voice rang out from the very back of the room.

A deep, masculine voice.

"Yeah, you're one of us. And we stick with our own."

Marissa grew very still, lowering both her hands to the lectern, steadying herself. Because even before her brain placed the voice, all her other senses had kicked in to tell her who was talking. Her stomach had begun doing flips, her legs shook and her eyes were filling up with moisture.

The boys also recognized the voice. They turned, the crowd parting to reveal Danny, who had apparently been hovering in a back corner, hidden by a dozen students.

"Hey, heard the great news, man."

"Way to go, Midas!"

"I'll be there with ya in twenty years."

The boys all called out their congratulations, and Danny nodded and smiled his appreciation for them. But his attention was focused on Mari. His stare focused directly on her face, he began to slowly walk toward the front of the lecture hall. Her heart thudded in time with his every step, her pulse roaring as she accepted the fact that he was really here.

"Sorry I'm late," he murmured when he reached the front of the room.

Licking her lips nervously, she whispered, "It's okay. I didn't have a very exciting topic to cover today."

"Taking risks, following your heart? I think that's a very good topic," he countered, a challenge in his voice.

"Actually, you're right. It is."

"So, what's your opinion?"

"On taking risks?"

"And following your heart."

She swallowed, murmuring, "I think if you care for someone it's not really taking a risk. It's just trusting in…"

"Fate?"

"Love."

His lids lowered slightly over those clear, gleaming eyes. Because she'd just admitted she loved him, even if he was the only one in the room who realized that.

"There's no place for cowardice when you love someone," she added, hoping he heard her certainty. Her voice didn't quaver, she didn't avert her stare. She wanted him to hear and *believe*. "All the old self-doubts and baggage can be pitched along the side of the road when it's *really* right. Because loving someone means trusting them, expecting only a bright and shiny future, not looking for reasons to bail when the going gets tough."

Around them, the students' voices had grown quiet, a nearly expectant hush falling over the hall, as if every one of them knew something important was happening between their two instructors.

"You really think it's that easy, letting go of a lifetime of doubt and pain?" he asked, stepping a little closer. Close enough that she could smell his aftershave, and feel his warmth.

She almost arched closer, needing to melt into that warmth, but instead answered, "Nothing worth having is easy. But I have no doubt I'm ready to do it."

A few whispers indicated their audience had realized things were getting personal. Because she'd said *I*.

Frankly, Marissa didn't care. She'd spent a miserable

two nights missing him, wishing she'd never let him leave, planning on how to, at the very least, ask for his forgiveness and at best see if he would be willing to give them another chance.

She saw the forgiveness on his face. Like all truly good men, Danny was capable of forgiving.

But the rest?

That might take a little more effort. And a little more bluntness.

"I love you, Danny."

A low rumble rolled through the room as every kid in it put their heads together to whisper.

She ignored everything but the man in front of her, who had sucked in one quick, audible inhalation at her bald pronouncement. "I love you, and I'm so sorry I let the fear take over."

He opened his mouth to speak, but she stopped him, knowing she had to say the rest.

"I allowed myself to forget who you are. Who I am. And who we are together." She reached for his hand. "I will never make that mistake again. Will you please give me a chance to make it up to you?"

His fingers tightening around hers, he stepped closer, looking down into her face with so much tenderness, she almost melted on the spot.

"Yes, I will," he promised, bending to brush his lips against hers, lightly, sweetly. Then he pulled away just far enough to say, "I love you, Mari."

The boys were clapping now, but she threw her arms around his neck, and drew him down for another, deeper kiss. He held her tightly, running his hands up and down her back, as if he wanted to make sure she was really there. Back where she belonged.

Where she hoped to always be.

"So, dude, does this mean she's going to Houston with you?" a voice asked.

They drew apart, but kept their arms around each other. Danny never took his eyes off her face as he replied, "I sure as hell hope so!"

Then, to her utter shock, he bent down, lowering himself to one knee in front of her. Of all her most optimistic hopes about how he might respond when she told him she loved him, and wanted to be with him, this was one moment she definitely had not envisioned.

"Well, what do you say, Mad-Mari? Do you think you can stand being an astronaut's wife?"

This time, she didn't even try to stop the tears flooding her eyes from rolling down her cheeks. Shaking her head, she replied, "I don't give a damn about being an astronaut's wife…I just want to be yours."

Epilogue

Sunday, 9/18/12, 06:00 a.m.
www.mad-mari.com/2012/09/18/married!
I'm married!

Can you believe it? Did you ever think you'd see the day? Me, a wife?!? Well, I know you've known you'd see the day over the past fifteen months, when I've been such a gooey bride-to-be, but before that? (Uh, FYI, for those of you who are new here, I really was something of a man-hater once upon a time. Read one of my books if you don't believe me.)

But all that was before Mr. Perfect.

Who is, of course, utterly perfect.

Our wedding day, while not perfect, was perfectly wonderful to us. Everything would have gone off without a hitch…had it not been for my new sister-in-law—let's call her J—going into labor just as the wedding march began to play!

I can tell you one thing—nobody's ever going to forget my wedding. I mean, how many people do you know who have heard the splash of a pregnant woman's water breaking halfway through the procession? I wish that funniest videos show was still on—the videographer caught the moment and it was absolutely priceless. J didn't look worried, she was pissed that she got amniotic fluid all over her new shoes! (I think the pastor was a little more pissed about the carpeting. Don't worry. We made a very nice donation to replace it.)

Anyway, J was her usual feisty, wonderful self, and insisted on sticking out the ceremony. We got her a chair, and she sat at the altar, trying to be quiet while she did a little hoo-hoo-ha-ha breathing. Right after we said our "I dos," her hubby (one of the grooms-men) whisked her into his arms and carried her out of the church to take her to the hospital. Swoon. My new mother-in-law (whom I adore) went, too, wanting to see the birth of her first grandchild, but everyone else partied with us at the reception, waiting for word.

We got the call just as we were cutting the cake— it's a boy! Welcome to the world little guy, I'm so excited to be your Aunt Mari.

Mr. Perfect and I didn't leave for our honeymoon right away. After the reception, the limo took us to the hospital to meet the new arrival—you should have seen the faces when we walked through the maternity ward, him absolutely drool-worthy in his tux, and me not too shabby in my OH, SO GORGEOUS gown.

Anyway, gotta wrap this up. It's now 6:00 a.m... I'm writing this right before we leave for the airport. Flight to Aruba leaves in three hours and I cannot wait to get the honeymoon started.

Oh, by the way, don't expect me to blog from there. I don't care if they do have internet service—I am completely disconnecting for the next week. I intend to enjoy every minute I can get with my new hubby, who's been working so hard at his new job for the past year! This is the first real break he's had since he started. (Can't get too specific, but let me just say—he's a real American hero.)

And he's my hero.

My Mr. Perfect.

See ya—

Mari

aka: Mrs. Perfect.

* * * * *

Harlequin® *Blaze*™

COMING NEXT MONTH

Available June 28, 2011

#621 BY INVITATION ONLY
Lori Wilde, Wendy Etherington, Jillian Burns

#622 TAILSPIN
Uniformly Hot!
Cara Summers

#623 WICKED PLEASURES
The Pleasure Seekers
Tori Carrington

#624 COWBOY UP
Sons of Chance
Vicki Lewis Thompson

#625 JUST LET GO…
Harts of Texas
Kathleen O'Reilly

#626 KEPT IN THE DARK
24 Hours: Blackout
Heather MacAllister

You can find more information on upcoming
Harlequin® titles, free excerpts and more at
www.HarlequinInsideRomance.com.

REQUEST YOUR FREE BOOKS!
2 FREE NOVELS PLUS 2 FREE GIFTS!

red-hot reads!

YES! Please send me 2 FREE Harlequin® Blaze® novels and my 2 FREE gifts (gifts are worth about $10). After receiving them, if I don't wish to receive any more books, I can return the shipping statement marked "cancel." If I don't cancel, I will receive 6 brand-new novels every month and be billed just $4.24 per book in the U.S. or $4.71 per book in Canada. That's a saving of at least 15% off the cover price. It's quite a bargain. Shipping and handling is just 50¢ per book in the U.S. and 75¢ per book in Canada.* I understand that accepting the 2 free books and gifts places me under no obligation to buy anything. I can always return a shipment and cancel at any time. Even if I never buy another book, the two free books and gifts are mine to keep forever.

151/351 HDN FC4T

Name _____ (PLEASE PRINT) _____

Address _____ Apt. # ____

City _____ State/Prov. _____ Zip/Postal Code ____

Signature (if under 18, a parent or guardian must sign)

Mail to the **Reader Service**:
IN U.S.A.: P.O. Box 1867, Buffalo, NY 14240-1867
IN CANADA: P.O. Box 609, Fort Erie, Ontario L2A 5X3

Not valid for current subscribers to Harlequin Blaze books.

Want to try two free books from another line?
Call 1-800-873-8635 or visit www.ReaderService.com.

* Terms and prices subject to change without notice. Prices do not include applicable taxes. Sales tax applicable in N.Y. Canadian residents will be charged applicable taxes. Offer not valid in Quebec. This offer is limited to one order per household. All orders subject to credit approval. Credit or debit balances in a customer's account(s) may be offset by any other outstanding balance owed by or to the customer. Please allow 4 to 6 weeks for delivery. Offer available while quantities last.

Your Privacy—The Reader Service is committed to protecting your privacy. Our Privacy Policy is available online at www.ReaderService.com or upon request from the Reader Service.

We make a portion of our mailing list available to reputable third parties that offer products we believe may interest you. If you prefer that we not exchange your name with third parties, or if you wish to clarify or modify your communication preferences, please visit us at www.ReaderService.com/consumerschoice or write to us at Reader Service Preference Service, P.O. Box 9062, Buffalo, NY 14269. Include your complete name and address.

HBII

USA TODAY *bestselling author B.J. Daniels*
takes you on a trip to Whitehorse, Montana,
and the Chisholm Cattle Company.

RUSTLED

Available July 2011 from Harlequin Intrigue.

As the dust settled, Dawson got his first good look at the rustler. A pair of big Montana sky-blue eyes glared up at him from a face framed by blond curls.

A woman rustler?

"You have to let me go," she hollered as the roar of the stampeding cattle died off in the distance.

"So you can finish stealing my cattle? I don't think so." Dawson jerked the woman to her feet.

She reached for the gun strapped to her hip hidden under her long barn jacket.

He grabbed the weapon before she could, his eyes narrowing as he assessed her. "How many others are there?" he demanded, grabbing a fistful of her jacket. "I think you'd better start talking before I tear into you."

She tried to fight him off, but he was on to her tricks and pinned her to the ground. He was suddenly aware of the soft curves beneath the jean jacket she wore under her coat.

"You have to listen to me." She ground out the words from between her gritted teeth. "You have to let me go. If you don't they will come back for me and they will kill you. There are too many of them for you to fight off alone. You won't stand a chance and I don't want your blood on my hands."

"I'm touched by your concern for me. Especially after you just tried to pull a gun on me."

"I wasn't going to shoot you."

Dawson hauled her to her feet and walked her the rest of the way to his horse. Reaching into his saddlebag, he pulled out a length of rope.

"You can't tie me up."

He pulled her hands behind her back and began to tie her wrists together.

"If you let me go, I can keep them from coming back," she said. "You have my word." She let out an unladylike curse. "I'm just trying to save your sorry neck."

"And I'm just going after my cattle."

"Don't you mean your boss's cattle?"

"Those cattle are mine."

"*You're* a Chisholm?"

"Dawson Chisholm. And you are…?"

"Everyone calls me Jinx."

He chuckled. "I can see why."

Bronco busting, falling in love…it's all in a day's work. Look for the rest of their story in

RUSTLED

Available July 2011 from Harlequin Intrigue wherever books are sold.

Copyright © 2011 by Barbara Heinlein

HIEXP0711R

Looking for a great Western read?

· · We have just the thing!

A Cowboy for Every Mood

Visit

www.HarlequinInsideRomance.com

for a sneak peek and exciting exclusives
on your favorite cowboy heroes.

Pick up next month's cowboy books
by some of your favorite authors:

Vicki Lewis Thompson
Carla Cassidy
B.J. Daniels
Rachel Lee
Christine Rimmer
Donna Alward
Cheryl St.John
And many more…

Available wherever books are sold.

ACFEM0611R